fragments

Jeffry W. Johnston

SIMON PULSE

New York London Toronto Sydney

For Janet Moore
With all my love forever and always

SIMON PULSE

An imprint of Simon & Schuster Children's Publishing Division
1230 Avenue of the Americas, New York, NY 10020
Copyright © 2007 by Jeffry W. Johnston
All rights reserved, including the right of reproduction in whole
or in part in any form.
SIMON PULSE and colophon are registered trademarks of Simon & Schuster, Inc.
Designed by Sammy Yuen Jr.
The text of this book was set in Meridien.
Manufactured in the United States of America
First Simon Pulse edition January 2007
2 4 6 8 10 9 7 5 3 1
Library of Congress Control Number 2006925164
ISBN-13: 978-1-4169-2486-9
ISBN-10: 1-4169-2486-8

ACKNOWLEDGMENTS

I have so many people I want to thank, starting with those who were around to read a lot of my earlier writing and attempts at writing. To **Joan VanderPutten**, **Beth Massie**, **Wayne Allen Sallee**, **Yvonne Navarro**, and **Brian Hodge**, thank you for those early years of encouragement.

More recently, a big thank-you to **Nancy Weigel**, **Stefanie DeKraft**, **Kate Heller-Burris**, **Janet Moore**, **Michael Poteet**, **Angela George**, **Frank McShane**, and **Sara Taylor** for reading various drafts of this book and offering input and insight. And a special thank-you to **Tracy Koontz** for all those two-man "writing group" lunches.

Thank you to my family for their love and support. Also, thank you so very much to my editor, **Jennifer Klonsky**, for her enthusiastic guidance and for making the process a lot of fun. I couldn't have asked for a better editor to help a nervous first-time novelist.

And finally, a deep, heartfelt thank-you to my agent, **Scott Treimel**, for taking me on at a time when I wasn't sure this was ever going to happen. For smoothing the rough edges and showing me how to take my writing to the next level, Scott, I can never thank you enough for all you have done for me.

CHAPTER 1

"Chase! It's seven thirty!"

I don't have to answer. Yet. Mom will call up again in a few minutes. She always does. I'd rather lie here for a while longer. In my own bed, my own room. I can just close my eyes. And breathe.

One-two-three-four. Two-four-six-eight.

Breathe.

Three-six-nine-twelve. Four-eight-twelve-sixteen.

Breathe.

Okay, now what is today? Monday, September thirteenth. A week and a half since the new school year started. My junior year. Six weeks since I got home from the hospital. Four and a half months since the car accident.

The car accident. Feeling as if something has come loose in my chest, I take a deeper breath this time.

"Chase?" My mother again. Mary Beth Farrell. An elementary school teacher before she became a pastor's wife, so she knows the importance of keeping to a schedule. "Are you awake? It's time to get up."

"I'm up!" I answer. "I'll be down in a minute!" That'll hold her for a while.

One-two-three-four. Two-four-six-eight.

Breathe.

Three-six-nine-twelve. Four-eight-twelve-sixteen.

Better.

I'm about to sit up, when in rushes a new memory from the night of the accident: Dan Butler and me laughing like two fools as he pumps foam from the keg because I forgot to tilt my cup the right way. The two of us laughing like it's the funniest thing to ever happen.

"That's the way it's going to come, Chase," Dr. McShane told me in the hospital. "Flashes of memory. Some clearer than others, and together they may never all make sense. But try to piece together what you can. Start meeting regularly with Dr. Braun. Remember, I'll be checking in with her."

The memory of Dan and me slowly fades. I take one more deep breath.

"Hey, get that lazy ass of yours out of bed."

"Ben!" I shout, opening my eyes.

"Shh." He leans over me and gives me that great smile of his. "I snuck in the front. You didn't hear me open your door?"

"No. I guess I was spacing." I sit up, feeling better, as always when my big brother's around. "I thought you were leaving town."

"I decided to wait. Decided I wanted to stay close for a while."

I hesitate, then ask, "Are you going to say something to Mom and Dad?"

He smirks. "What do you think?"

"I think, maybe . . . I don't know, they seem different. Like they really want to try and understand, you know?"

"Understand you, maybe. Not me." He backs up, and, I'm afraid he's going to leave. He starts pacing around the room like a caged animal. "It's better if they think I left town. Okay?"

"Yeah, sure. So where are you staying?"

"You don't need to know."

"Why?"

"So you won't accidentally tell Mom and Dad."

"You don't trust me?"

Ben stops pacing. "It's just, the less you know the better." He cuffs me on the cheek. "Hell, you know I trust you."

"But you'll be around for a while?"

"Yeah. For a while."

"That's great."

"But let's keep that between you and me."

"Sure."

"Don't you think you should get dressed?" he asks.

Jumping off the bed, I cross to the closet to get out some clothes.

"This house is decent," Ben says. "Another parsonage?"

"This church doesn't give a housing allowance," I tell him.

"You know which house I liked? When I was . . . ten, I think. So you were eight. We had a really big room. We took that huge quilt Mom made and hung it like a tent. Pretended we were secret agents and that was our headquarters."

"There's an extra room . . ."

"That won't happen."

"They might—"

"What? Forgive me? That's not happening either. Get it through your head, Chase—I'm not coming back." I hang my head, and he comes toward me, tousles my hair. "To live here, I mean. Of course I'll come see you. But you can't let Mom and Dad know. It's gotta stay a secret."

I look up and nod. "I promise."

"My sneaking into the house is risky, though. Maybe we can meet some other place."

"Like where?"

"We'll figure it out."

"I wish I was more like you," I blurt out.

"You mean, an ex-convict?"

"You know what I mean. Tough. Boy of steel."

"What?"

"When you pretended to be Superboy up on the roof that time. Remember? That's what you called yourself."

"I did?" He grins.

"You were eleven. You broke your arm."

I want to say more. I want to tell him I wish he and Mom and Dad weren't mad at one another so he could live here. I want to say again how different things would be if he came back.

"When are you gonna tell me what it was like?" I ask.

"You're too young."

"You're only two years older than me—"

"Breakfast is on the table, Chase!" Dad's turn this time. The Reverend Matthew Farrell.

"I'm coming!" I call out, and put on my shoes.

"Listen," Ben says. "You go down first, and I'll sneak out the front door while you distract them. I'll wait and walk to school with you, if you want."

"Sure."

At the bottom of the stairs I glance up over my shoulder at my closed bedroom door. My father's at the kitchen table.

"There he is," Dad says, looking up from his paper, grinning. "Thought we'd have to send a search party upstairs. How are you this morning? Are you okay?" Dad asks that a lot since I came home.

"Yeah," I say, and watch him relax.

"Good. Sit down and eat. We've got cereal, we've got fruit—"

"Cereal's fine." I'm listening for noise from the living room. Maybe that's the front door I hear, clicking quietly shut.

"Here, you want the sports section?" He hands over a section of folded newspaper.

"Why?"

"Baseball. The pennant races."

"Morning." Mom comes in all prom-queen pretty and bends over to kiss me on the cheek. "You look tired, Chase. Did you sleep all right?" She pours herself a cup of coffee. "Why don't we drive you to school today? It's on the way to my Women's Fellowship meeting at Mrs. Brogan's house, and your Dad's got a couple of hospital visits."

"I'd rather walk," I tell her quietly.

"You always do, but it's hot this morning, and I thought . . ." She lets it trail off.

"What?" I ask.

"Maybe you'd like a break."

"A break . . . ?"

"It's two miles to school. You don't even take the bus."

"I like to walk."

"Exercise is a good thing, Chase," Dad says. "Nothing wrong with exercise. If he wants to walk, Mary Beth . . ." He waves as if he's settled the "issue" and returns to his paper. Mom takes a sip of her coffee, standing by the counter.

"It's not because of the accident," I tell them. "I like walking."

"Okay," Dad responds. "That's okay."

"I don't remember the accident. How can cars scare me?"

"Okay," Dad repeats. His mantra. "Maybe it's not important you remember anything. Maybe it's even for the better."

"Is that what Dr. Braun thinks?" Mom asks, still standing, holding her cup tightly with both hands as though it might slip otherwise. "That it's not important whether you remember?"

"I don't know," I answer. *One-two-three-four.*

"Not that you have to tell us," Dad says, fussing with

his paper. "We understand what goes on between you and your therapist is private."

"She might think it's not important." *Two-four-six-eight.* "I'm not sure. I've only been seeing her a few weeks." Breathe.

"But you go twice a week," Mom says.

"Excuse me." Dad stands. "I need to get some things for today." To Mom, "Will you be ready soon?"

"I have to get some things too, for my meeting." Mom pours her full cup of coffee into the sink. "You haven't poured your cereal, Chase."

"I will."

"Do you have time?" she asks. "If we drive you, you'll have more time. You can have two bowls and some fruit—"

"I'm fine!" Silence. They stare at me. Study me. Ladies and gentlemen, behind the glass wall, witness the species known as teenager. Notice how, even at sixteen, he is unable to do the day-to-day things you and I take for granted.

"I'll take a banana with me," I manage to say.

"Sure," Dad says. "Okay." Turning to his wife, "I'll be in my study until you're ready." Back to me. "Have a good day, Chase."

"If you change your mind and want a ride home," Mom says, not one to give up, "I'll have my cell."

"I see Dr. Braun today after school."

"Oh, that's right." She tries a halfhearted smile. They exit the kitchen, leaving me to my breakfast.

I wish I hadn't shouted at them. Now they're probably talking about me.

Glancing at the clock on the stove, I see it's time to go.

The house we live in is a split-level, with two bedrooms and the extra room on the top floor, and the living room, dining room, and kitchen on the middle floor. Down the stairs from the kitchen is the family room. As I go through the living room on my way out the door, I pass the display on the mantel. First, there's a picture of Mom, Dad, and me taken in front of the church right after he was hired. Next to it is my school picture from last year.

There's Mom and Dad's wedding photo. Opposite are photos of their parents—Dad's passed away before I was born, Mom's when I was too young to remember. The next picture is of my father, posing with his older brother, who was twelve years older, and whom he idolized. Uncle Julius died when I was ten. My mother is an only child.

There's not a single one of Ben anywhere in the house.

On the wall above the mantel is the family crucifix. Passed down from my dad's grandfather to his father to

Dad. I'll be expected to take it when I get married, I guess. It's Dad's prized possession. Jesus hanging on the cross, blood flowing from the crown of thorns clinging to his head and the nails piercing his hands and feet.

I'm never able to walk past it. The eyes latch on and follow me around the room.

I stop.

First I check to make sure the figure isn't cracked or broken. Because I know how upset Dad would be if something happened to it. Then I count—*one-two-three-four* . . . *two-four-six-eight* . . . up to four-eight-twelve-sixteen. Sometimes it works, and I move on. More often, I have to start over. Do it again. *One-two-three-four.* Several times.

It takes twice this time. Then I'm able to leave the house.

CHAPTER 2

Things were better for us at the last church. Before getting hired there, Dad had done nothing but interim pastoring, uprooting his family five times in eight years. His first full-time position was at a large congregation, and Dad was well respected. His sermons thundered down from the pulpit, and people respected him and, maybe, feared him too. He enjoyed the responsibility of being the one everyone came to for spiritual advice. On Sunday mornings everyone listened and thanked him afterward for his wisdom and took the message from the day's sermon home to chew over with their Sunday afternoon dinner. There was plenty of money in the collection plate every week, and the church thrived.

Then Ben started getting into trouble. When things really went bad and Ben was sent to the youth detention center, Dad decided we had to move. He couldn't be expected to preach, to lead, to be a spokesman for God, and continue to have the respect of a congregation aware of sin in his own family.

So he found this church. A lot smaller. But a new beginning.

Then came the car accident. With me the only survivor. In fact, with hardly a scratch on me. So maybe my parents had every right to think that, after some time had passed—after the funerals and testimonials and grief counselors the school provided, and the prayer chain Dad had helped organize in conjunction with all the local churches—things were ready to settle down.

But then I had to ruin things with my little stunt with my father's straightedge. My second attempt at offing myself, actually.

The first time, nobody noticed. Not that I'd even planned it to begin with.

It just sort of happened.

I was alone in the house, standing in my underwear, staring at my reflection in the bathroom mirror, and I heard a voice say, *"Do it."* Just like that. And without thinking, really, I gave the glass a good wallop. I could have used one of the shards to slit my wrist. But instead of breaking into smaller pieces that would fall out like I'd envisioned, the mirror developed two long cracks. I hit it a couple more times, but the cracks kept multiplying until there must have been fifty different cracks, and still not a single piece fell out.

When Dad got home from the church and asked me why the mirror was smashed, I told him I'd slipped. He shook his head, patted me on the back, and said how lucky I was I didn't hurt myself.

After several weeks had passed and I hadn't heard the voice again, I decided it had been nothing more than a weird accident. I probably had slipped.

When the voice returned, it was pretty insistent. I was in the bathroom, and this time it screamed at me, *"Do it! DO IT!"* and I just did it.

The blade was fresh. The cuts took forever to bleed. Found out later, if you want results, slice the veins lengthwise so the blood really flows. My parents got home from their church board meeting, found me on the bathroom floor, and called the ambulance.

I managed to lose enough blood to scare the hell out of them before I was stabilized in the emergency room. Dad did not say I was lucky this time. I was given a "psych consult," followed by a trip to the psychiatric wing of the hospital. The way insurance companies are, you've got to be more than just suicidal to stay beyond a week. They want padded-cell material.

Which I was.

Two months later they let me out.

I don't see Ben anywhere. Disappointed, I start walking to school alone.

It was actually Dr. McShane's idea. "I want you to promise me," he told me the day before my release, "that you'll walk every day."

"Why?" I ask.

"Consider it time for yourself. Time when you don't have to answer to anybody. My best thoughts come when I'm walking."

"Really?"

"Yeah." McShane smiles. That smile made me feel safe.

"Walk every day," he says, "even if it's only ten minutes."

I make sure not to step on the cracks in the sidewalk. Can't really say why. It's just better not to take chances.

"Did you ever hear of survivor guilt?" Dr. McShane asked me once.

"Sure. I saw a movie about it. *Fearless.*"

"Yeah?"

"This guy survives a plane crash. Not a scratch on him."

"Sounds familiar."

"He starts doing weird things, and weird things start happening. He eats strawberries even though he's deathly allergic to them, but nothing happens. He purposely crashes his car into a wall and survives."

"You like this movie?"

"Yeah."

"About a guy trying to kill himself," Dr. McShane says.

"That's part of it. So what?"

"I'm just trying to make connections. That's my job. Helping you make sense of this scattered stuff. Do you know what I mean?"

"I'm not sure," I say.

"It's not important right now." He smiles. "You enjoy movies, don't you?

"Yeah."

"Ever think you might like acting in them?"

"I don't know."

"Ever think about being a minister like your dad?"

"Hell, no," I scoff.

"What's wrong with being a minister?

"You gotta give sermons every Sunday. My dad sweats blood over them. And everyone expects so much. If they want him, he's supposed to just drop what he's doing and come running."

I think about my sessions with Dr. McShane a lot.

"Everything we talked about in here, you'll be

able to talk about with Dr. Braun," he told me during our last session.

"I don't want to."

"You didn't want to talk to me at first." For four days I had refused to get out of bed except to use the bathroom.

"I'm different now," I say.

"Exactly."

"Why can't I keep coming to see you?"

"Because you can't once you leave."

"Then I don't want to leave."

"You have to. It's time to go."

In a quieter voice. "But it's safe here."

After a moment he says, "Your real work's out there, Chase. Not here. This is only a stopgap."

"What if the voice starts telling me to 'do it' again?"

"Have you heard it here in the hospital?"

"No."

"How many times before you came here?"

"Twice."

"The two times you tried to kill yourself."

"Yeah."

"Do you feel now like you want to kill yourself?"

"No. But maybe I should go back on medication. Just in case."

Dr. McShane leans forward. "Chase, look at me." I do, peering into steely gray eyes. "If I honestly thought you were in trouble, I wouldn't release you. Believe me."

"I still don't get why I can't come here to see you," I mutter.

He sits back. "Think of this place as triage. You get hurt, you go to an emergency room and they treat your wounds and send you home. Then another doctor takes over your treatment, and he becomes the one you depend on until you get well. I'm the ER doctor." He leans in. "All I did here was treat the wound. It's time for you to work on the healing."

Now as I walk to school, I hear something.

Laughter.

Thinking I hear Ben, I look back and step off the curb.

A new sound. Screeching brakes.

And a voice. "Hey, kid, are you trying to kill yourself?"

I look over and see a car has stopped just a few yards from me. Not that close, really, but my heart's racing.

The guy behind the wheel, beet-faced and angry, is leaning out his window. "Well, you gonna get out of the way?"

Then his gaze softens, and he asks, "Are you okay, kid?"

I hear him, but I'm seeing someone else.

"Are you okay, kid?"

A man in a cop uniform. Asking that same question.

"Look, just step back on the curb. So I know this isn't

an insurance scam." Before gunning the engine and zooming off down the road, he shoots me the finger.

I remain still, waiting for my heart to slow down.

One-two-three-four. Two-four-six-eight. Breathe.

What made me do that? What distracted me?

I hear it again. *Laughter.* It's not Ben. It's another new memory.

Everybody in the car is drunk. Except Angie behind the wheel. She wasn't at the party; she came to pick us up. The laughter is from behind me. Dan and Sara and Jay. I'm in the front passenger seat. Is Angie laughing too? Was that what happened? I told a stupid joke and everybody was so busy laughing that no one noticed the other car swing from around the corner and swerve into our lane?

I close my eyes and try to picture it. But my head is like a giant cavern, and the space inside is dark and endless, the shapes I see only shadows.

"Hey, kiddo, are you all right?"

I open my eyes. "Ben! Where were you?"

"Sorry. I was in the back, looking the house over, when you came out. You were already several blocks away. Didn't you hear me calling you?"

"No."

"You scared the shit out of me when you stepped in front of that car. Are you okay?"

"I thought you'd changed your mind."

He smiles. "I promised I'd walk with you, didn't I? Let's go."

I always feel better when my brother's around. There's nobody in the world I can talk to the same way. It's always been like that.

We reach Westfield High and Ben waves good-bye. And I'm already thinking, *When will I see him again?*

CHAPTER 3

Heading down the hall toward first period, Heather and Kyle from drama class cut me off. "Hi, Chase," Kyle says. "We want to ask you something."

"What?" I ask.

"You're auditioning for the role of the Common Man, right?"

I look at them. "Huh?"

"Tryouts for *A Man for All Seasons* this week," Heather says. "Remember?"

"I haven't thought about it, really."

"Sure you haven't." Kyle shakes his head.

"Why do you want to know?" I ask, a little annoyed.

"I want the role of Thomas More. But if you're auditioning for it, I might as well forget it."

"Well, I haven't decided."

"You'd better start," Heather says. "I heard Mr. Hannah sold Principal Jarvis on this play because of the talent he told him he has available this year. I'm sure he meant more than Kyle and me. He meant you, too."

"I doubt it," I tell her. What I leave unsaid is why. Last spring we were doing *Godspell* and I had the lead, when four performances into the seven-performance run of the show, I did my solo act with the razor blade and they had to use my understudy. I heard the new Jesus forgot a lot of lines and missed his blocking. He's not in drama this year.

"Everybody knows the Common Man is really the main role," Kyle notes.

"If you want," Heather says, leaning into me, "I can run lines with you during lunch or after school."

I look at her. Heather is gorgeous and talented and gets big roles. She's gone out of her way recently to show how kind and understanding she can be.

Also, we have a history.

"I've got to get going," Kyle says. "I've got first period in one of the science labs." Calling back over his shoulder he says, "Can you let me know by eighth period?" He then makes a hurried exit.

"I'll walk with you, Chase," Heather offers. "My first class is on the way."

"You don't have to."

"I want to."

As we go down the hall, she gives me that concerned look she's so good at, and asks, "So how are you really doing?" As if all I have to do is unburden my soul to her to be saved.

"I'm fine."

"You can be honest with me, you know."

"I'm fine, Heather."

She stares as if she doesn't believe me. But she lets it go.

There isn't anybody here I feel like talking to about it.

And it doesn't help that I hear other kids talking.

"He's got some balls, coming back here."

"Makes you wonder what happened in that car, if he had to cut himself."

"I heard Angie was seat-belted and still went through the windshield. They had to use dental records for ID."

"Chase, I asked you a question," I hear Heather say. "What do you think of Darla Prince?"

"Who?" I ask.

"The new girl in drama."

"I haven't thought anything about her."

"I think she's weird. And pretentious as hell."

"How do you figure that? She doesn't talk much."

"So you have noticed her."

I don't say anything.

"I think she's got an attitude," Heather continues, rolling her eyes. "I tried to talk to her. She completely ignored me."

"She's new. Maybe she's shy."

"If she was shy, she wouldn't dress the way she does."

"Maybe."

"Why do you think she dresses like that? Do you think she's a dyke?"

Looking at her, I bump right into Kevin Harris.

"Whoa," he says, throwing his hands out to keep me from stumbling over him.

"S-sorry," I stutter. "I didn't see you there."

"It's all right," he says. "Don't worry about it. You doing okay?"

"Uh, yeah." Everybody keeps *asking* that.

"Good. That's good."

Kevin Harris is a wrestler. Built stocky and muscular and close to the ground. A serious guy, really, not like a lot of wrestling jocks.

He's also Angie's boyfriend.

Was.

"Can I talk to you a minute, Farrell?" Behind him are buddies from the team. Lars and Mitch. They watch with suspicion.

"I've gotta go to class—"

"Just for a minute. I was just wondering—"

"I still can't tell you anything."

"Don't freak out on me. I just wanna talk."

"But I don't remember anything."

"Nothing?"

"I'm sorry."

"Okay, that's all right," Kevin says. "Really. But I was thinking, maybe . . . I don't know . . . after school today, I'd buy you a burger or something. Just you and me. Relaxed, you know? It might help you."

"Kevin, if I remembered anything, I'd tell you."

"Would you?"

I stare at him.

"Look, you're the only one who knows what happened. Meet me after school."

"I can't. I've got somewhere to go."

"Tomorrow, then." Pushing. Edging up to me.

One-two-three-four.

"Come on, Chase—"

"He said he'll tell you if he remembers anything," Heather pipes in.

"You stay out of this." Kevin points at her.

"Big tough jock," she sneers.

"He told you to stay out of it!" Lars growls from behind Kevin.

"Ooh, what are you gonna do? Put me in a head-lock?"

"Theatre freak. Lesbo—"

"That's enough!" Kevin orders.

Two-four-six-eight. Breathe. *Three-six-nine-twelve.*

"Hey, look at him!" Mitch says, pointing. At me.

They all stop to stare. Looking back at them, I open my mouth to talk, but nothing comes out. It feels as if there's something in my throat. I can feel my hands trembling, and I shove them into my pockets.

"What the hell's wrong with him?" Lars utters.

"Chase, are you all right?" Heather asks.

"I'm okay," I say finally, my throat like sandpaper. "I'm fine."

"What is this?" Mitch scoffs. "One of those weird theatre exercises?"

"Shut up!" Kevin snaps, and Mitch backs up, offended.

The next bell rings, signaling two minutes until first period. "Some day soon we're gonna do this," Kevin says, backing up. "I've got to, Farrell. You'd do the same if you were me." He turns and walks away, his friends staring back at me as they follow.

"Come on, Chase, it's all right," Heather says. "I'll walk with you to your first class."

"You don't need to."

"I want to."

"Really, I'm fine."

"Let me—"

"Heather! I'm okay. Please!"

She stares at me, hurt, but braves a smile. "All right," she says. "I'll see you in drama."

Damn it. I could have handled that better.

Like I said, we have a history.

I turn and watch Kevin, still in view down the hall. I would tell him if I remembered what happened.

The bell signals the beginning of first period. Now when I walk into class, everybody's going to be staring.

It took me a long time to remember *anything* about the accident. I was told the police found me walking four blocks away. I had cuts and bruises, but nothing serious, which, considering the car from the picture in the paper, was something for Ripley's Believe It or Not! They said I was walking in a very determined manner. They also said I was legally drunk. But they knew I hadn't been driving.

A woman saw the accident from her living room window and said she saw someone fall from the front passenger door at the time of impact. The cops sat me on the curb and brought a paramedic. Then the ambulance came. I don't remember the wreckage. I only saw the front page.

I remember Dan Butler picking me up for the party. In the back seat were Sara Buchanan and Jay Kerrigan. Dan's friends. Dan was in last year's fall production of *Brigadoon*, something he did for a kick, he told me. It was my first show at Westfield, having just moved here the summer before, and I surprised people by landing the part of Harry Beaton, the third male lead. Dan and I were both new to the Westfield theatre scene, so maybe that's why we became friends even though he hung out with the motorheads and I eventually settled in with the drama group. And we remained friends even after Dan decided not to audition for *Godspell*.

When we got to the party, there was plenty of beer, and the last thing I remember is somebody handing me a cup almost as soon as I walked in. Everything was a blur after that until the cop asked me, "Are you all right?" Until I started talking about it with Dr. McShane and, later, Dr. Braun.

I guess it was me who had the idea to call Angie to pick us up when none of us was sober enough to drive. Her dad, who had answered the phone, couldn't say whose voice he heard asking for his daughter. As for her coming to get us, that's how Angie is. Was. The kind who'd come at one in the morning to be a designated driver. Even for an ex-boyfriend.

According to reports, the driver of the other car was drunk and alone and, judging from the lack of skid marks, came around the curve and hit us full force, at about eighty-five miles an hour. He died five hours later.

Only Dan stayed alive long enough to make it into the ambulance after they used the jaws of life to get him out. He died in front of the ER.

The doctors kept me for twenty-four hours for observation, until they declared my memory loss had no *physical* cause.

CHAPTER 4

Before each session Dr. Braun says, "I'm gonna smoke, do you mind? I know—it's a filthy habit." Then she opens the window behind her and lights up the foulest-smelling cigarette.

This afternoon's session is no different. She leans back, looking at me in the strange way she does, her chin pressed down against her chest, her eyes raised up and peering at me over the top of her granny glasses, her fingers interlocked over a pretty good-size gut. I've never asked her age, but I guess she's in her fifties, and I don't think she ever won any beauty contests when she was young.

"So how was school today?" she asks. "Any easier?" This is our ninth session.

"I don't know. Maybe a little."

"People acting like maybe they can't trust you?"

"Yeah."

"What about your parents?"

"My dad keeps asking me if I'm okay," I grumble. "I think he's worried I might explode or something. Sometimes Mom asks me questions about my sessions with you."

"What do you tell her?"

"Not much. I think she feels they're a waste of time."

"That's a shame. Anything happen at school today?"

I tell her about Kevin Harris.

"Angie's boyfriend."

"Yeah," I say. "He thinks if he buys me a burger, I'll remember the accident."

"If only it was that easy." She takes a drag off her cigarette, then holds it between her fingers. A long ash has begun growing on the end of it.

"I understand why he's asking."

"Why is he, do you think?"

"He wants to know what her last moments were like," I say. "Like that'll help him."

"Do you think it will?"

"I don't know." She inhales, and the ash looks like it's ready to fall off any second. Her features are scarred from what must have been a major acne problem when she was a teenager, and her hair always seems in need of brushing. All of which doesn't bother me as much now as when I met her.

"What did you tell him?" She taps the ash into her cupped palm and leans over to empty it into an ashtray on a side table.

"That I can't remember."

"Is that still true?"

I look at her, not answering. She waits. Dr. Braun loves silence. Sometimes I think if I tried keeping my mouth shut the whole session, she'd be content to just sit and watch me. A forty-five-minute game of chicken.

The time I met her—my first appointment—I heard "Shit, damn, piss" coming from the other side of the door into her office as I walked into the waiting room. As I sat down, she came bursting through the door sucking her finger, looked at me, and asked, "You Chase Farrell?"

Taken aback, I nodded.

"Come on in." I followed her into a cluttered office, books stuffed onto shelves built into the wall, files with papers protruding out the sides piled high on a cheap desk with cigarette burns visible in the wood. Next to it was a small wastebasket filled with trash.

"Have a seat," she says. "Could you hear me cursing? Sorry about that. I was trying to hang a picture and hammered my damn finger." I don't see a picture, hanging or otherwise, but say nothing. Walking over to a stained coffeemaker, she picks up the half-filled pot and asks, "Do you drink coffee?"

"No."

"Good boy. I don't either." She puts it back down and pulls out a pack of cigarettes. "I'm gonna smoke, do you mind? I know—it's a filthy habit." She opens the window, sits, and our first session begins.

"So, what brings you here today?"

"Don't you know?" I ask, wondering if this is a trick question.

"You mean from just looking at you?"

"I mean from talking to Dr. McShane. And my parents."

"They told me a little. You were in the hospital for two months. Prior to that you were in a car accident. You survived; everyone else died."

"Yeah." I feel a lump in my throat.

"You weren't driving, right?"

"That's right."

"So it wasn't your fault."

"I can't remember."

"Yeah, Dr. McShane mentioned that."

"What else did he tell you?"

"I'd rather hear it from you."

"What?"

"What it is that's bothering you."

"Who said anything's bothering me?"

She looks at me and sighs. Then, rising, she crosses to her desk and picks the top file off the pile. The pile teeters, but doesn't fall. "Your father's a minister. Your mother's a former teacher. And you have a brother in a youth detention center."

"What does that have to do with anything?" I snap.

She peers at me. "I'm not sure. You tell me."

"Nothing. That's not why I'm here."

"Oh." She closes the file. "Why are you here?"

I peer back at her, trying to figure out if this is a game. She doesn't move, other than to bring the cigarette to her mouth.

"Because I tried to kill myself."

"Is that why you *want* to be here? To talk about trying to kill yourself?"

"I never said I *wanted* to be here."

"Oh. You're here because . . . ?"

"Dr. McShane told me to come."

"I see. You were forced. And you're mad because I'm not him."

I don't say anything. She stares. Like God watching me.

"I guess . . . I need to be here."

"I think that's right," she says.

We both say nothing for a long time. "So how do we do this?" I ask finally.

"Do you think you can handle my not being Dr. McShane?"

I waver, then nod. "He told me you're good."

"Well, I guess that's for you to find out."

"Okay."

"Tell me how you've been feeling."

After a minute, "Nervous. Uneasy."

"Apprehensive?"

I nod.

"Like people are constantly watching you?"

"Yeah."

"Makes sense."

I waver again, then blurt out, "Do you think I should try to remember what happened the night of the accident?"

"You don't remember anything?"

"No, not really."

"We could start there. But I'm not promising your memory will come back. Maybe bits and pieces."

"Dr. McShane said 'flashes.'"

"What is it *you* want to accomplish?"

"I . . . I don't know."

"Come on," she pushes. "You must have some expectations."

After a moment I tell her, "I'd like things to be normal. To get back to normal, I mean."

"Hmm. That's a tough one. We'll have to see about that." She nods. "Let's talk about a schedule."

Now it's September thirteenth, and I've been seeing her for over a month. Her question—"Is that still true?"—hangs in the air. And now she adds, "Do you remember something new?"

"Dan Butler and I drinking from a keg. Drunk."

"This would be at the party, then."

"Yeah. And something else. Laughter."

"Laughter?"

"In the car. I think maybe right before the accident, I told a joke. And everybody started laughing."

"Okay."

"I think maybe . . . that's why she got distracted."

"Angie?"

"Yeah. That's why she didn't see the car in time. Because she was laughing at my joke."

"You remember her laughing? Then the car hitting you?"

"Well, not exactly."

Dr. Braun picks up a spiral notebook, flips some pages, and says, "There was a witness, if you remember. A woman looking from the front window of her house. She says the car that hit you came from around that corner so fast there was no way Angie had time to react."

"Yeah, I heard that."

"It's good you fell out, or you might have been killed too."

"I guess."

She flips the notebook back onto the side table. "You really want it to be your fault, huh?"

"Why else can't I remember?"

"Why do *you* think you can't?"

I look down at the floor. "Because I feel guilty."

"You probably do. That's not uncommon with something like this, you know." She taps another stem of ash into her palm and tosses it into the ashtray. Some of it misses and lands on the floor. "It's called survivor guilt."

"*Fearless*," I mumble.

"Pardon?"

"*Fearless*. It's a movie I saw a couple of times."

"I saw that one. Pretty good movie. A bit overblown." She inhales one last time then grinds the cigarette out. "That's right, Dr. McShane told me you like movies. What's your favorite film?"

"*To Kill a Mockingbird*," I tell her.

"Great movie. Gregory Peck's wonderful in that." She leans toward me. "Remember the climax? Boo Radley saves Scout and Jem. But in the process the guy who attacked them is killed. And even though the sheriff knows it was Boo who did it, protecting the children, he says the official report will be that the guy 'fell on his knife.'"

"And the point is?" I ask after a period of silence.

"That sometimes it's just about doing what you can to survive."

"You think I did something to Angie just to save myself?"

"No, damn it, that's not what I meant." She shakes her head. "Never mind. Maybe that was a bad example." Dr. Braun starts to tap out a new cigarette, but changes her mind and places the pack back on the table. "There's a reason why you continue to block the accident. Part of you wants to know, but there's a bigger part that doesn't, and that's the part of you I'm more interested in."

"What do you mean?"

"Why *don't* you want to remember? People are in accidents all the time. Serious accidents where other people die. Unless there's something like a head injury involved, they don't usually forget."

"So?"

"I think there's more to this than just the accident and, eventually, I want to talk about what that is."

"I don't know what you're talking about."

"You don't have to right now. Just think about it, okay? Maybe something will come to you."

"Look at me, Chase! I'm Superboy!"

"That look on your face . . . Something come to mind?"

"No."

"I think yes."

"No."

"Come on, don't hide it from me. There shouldn't be any secrets here."

She stares and starts playing her silent game. I wonder how much time is left in the session. The clock is placed so only she can see it.

The silence stretches out. So does my anxiety, and I abruptly change the subject. "I saw Ben today."

She frowns, but says, "I thought you told me he was going to do some traveling."

"He changed his mind. He wants to stay in the area for a while. To be with me."

"Well, that's nice. I'll bet your parents are happy."

"They don't know."

"He's not staying at your house?"

"No. He and my parents don't get along. I told you that."

"Because of what he did to put himself in jail?"

"Yeah."

"Why don't they want to forgive him? Your dad's a minister; I thought he was in the forgiving business."

"I guess it's complicated."

"I'll bet. But Ben wants to be near you. Why, to keep an eye on you?"

"Sure. He wants to protect me."

"From what?"

"I don't know what you're—"

"What do you need him to protect you from?"

One-two-three-four. "Nothing. There's nothing—"

"You said 'protect.'"

Two-four-six-eight. Breathe.

"Chase?"

"Because I'm his little brother."

"And big brothers protect little brothers?"

"Sure."

"And Ben always protects you."

"Yeah." *Three-six-nine-twelve.*

"How about when you were growing up?"

"Of course." *Four-eight-twelve-sixteen.*

"You seem nervous. Are you okay?"

"Yeah."

"There's nothing you're not telling me, right? Nothing you need protection from?"

"No."

"But there is some protecting going on here."

"What do you mean?"

"You're protecting yourself. Or your mind is. By blocking out the accident."

I stare at her a moment, then look away. "Everybody in that car died, except me," I whisper.

"Yes," she responds, her voice, for once, gentle.

"I was in the passenger seat. Angie died right next to me."

Dr. Braun says nothing. Watching.

"And I don't remember it. But I should."

"Maybe you will," she says. "We'll see."

The silence that follows is actually a blessing. My breathing gets easier.

"I guess it's almost time, huh?" I say then. "Don't you have somebody else—"

"How long have you been obsessive-compulsive, Chase?"

"Obsessive what?" Suddenly the room feels close.

"Compulsive. The obsessive need to perform some task. It can show up in a lot of different ways. The need to wash one's hands over and over, or clicking lights on and off. Or counting. That's what you're doing, right? When things start feeling out of control, you count, using some kind of established pattern until you feel okay again."

"I . . . I don't know what you—"

"Come on, you don't have to hide it from me. It's okay. I picked up on it during our first session, actually. Sometimes your lips move a tiny bit when you're doing it."

"My lips?"

"And your foot taps on the floor. You're probably not even aware of it. Four taps, pause, four taps, pause."

"I don't want to talk about it."

"Is there anything else you do? Things you feel you *have* to do?"

I say nothing.

"I had a client once who had a compulsive need to check the burners on his stove whenever he walked past it, even though he hadn't turned them on. An associate of mine knew someone who always had to lead with her right foot when she walked, or it spoiled her whole day. There are a lot of ways—" She stops and frowns. "I'm sorry. I ambushed you. That really wasn't my intention." Leaning in she says, "Look, as far as I'm concerned, whatever helps you get through the day right now is fine by me. I just didn't want you to think you were pulling a fast one. Our relationship in here should be based on honesty."

"I can't believe . . . ," I mumble. "If you could figure it out . . ."

"You wonder if others can tell? I doubt it." She winks. "I'm a professional, remember."

I look at her, and feel found out. Exposed.

"It's time to stop for today. I'll see you Thursday."

"Huh?"

"Thursday," she says.

I just look at her.

"What? Did you think I was going to tell you not to come back?"

I shrug, and she smiles. "Can't get rid of me that easily, Chase."

In a bit of a daze, but also inexplicably relieved, I walk out.

CHAPTER 5

I walk into my house through the back door and find Dad sitting at the kitchen table, his back to me. He's got a yellow writing pad next to him and a couple of pens. It could be his next sermon; he likes to get an early start. Or maybe he's preparing for the weekly Bible study he and Mom lead. I notice he's got a Bible in his hands.

He must not have heard me, because he doesn't move, and I just watch him for a moment.

People in this church don't know what a thunderbolt he used to be behind the pulpit. He wasn't one of those Bible-thumping "You're gonna go to hell if you don't turn to Jesus" kind of preachers. He knows his stuff, and he used to like to challenge people with his sermons. Make them think about their actions and what they should do to be better Christians. He used to love saying that Jesus set very high standards when he died so bloody up on the cross, and we must strive to attain them. It's probably what made him so attractive to congregations in need of an interim minister. Someone who could keep the congregation's blood flowing while the search was on for a full-time pastor. Good for the short-term, but after a while even the staunchest Christian can get burned out.

His passion fascinated me when I was younger. And frightened me too. It never bothered Ben, though. He laughed, and found all the hallelujahs people used to shout Dad's way absolutely hilarious.

It's been a long time since I've heard him give a sermon like that, though.

I notice he hasn't turned a page of the Bible since I walked in. Rather, he seems lost in thought as he stares at the page, and as I move toward him, he suddenly turns and sees me, shielding the book with his body as he quickly closes it.

"Here you are," he says, putting the Bible down and running a hand across his eyes that I realize now look a little red. "I've been thinking about the scripture for next Sunday. Didn't hear you come in. How was school?"

"Okay," I say with a shrug.

"Good. That's good. Must be getting into the swing of things by now. Hey, auditions for *A Man for All Seasons* must be coming up. Have you decided what role you're trying out for?"

"No, I haven't," I tell him.

"I guess you'd better make up your mind soon. Personally, I think you'd be great playing Thomas More. Such a noble figure."

"Some people think the Common Man is really the main role."

"The . . . the what?"

"He narrates and also plays a couple of other parts, like More's servant."

"No, Chase, not the servant. Thomas More. It's a great role."

"Dad, I need to—"

"I'm so glad your teacher has decided to do this play," he continues, smiling now. "It's a challenge for you kids. Other plays you've done, you've been good, but this one . . . Thomas More was a man of conviction. The way you love movies, you must have seen the film version."

"In school a couple of years ago."

"My brother took me to see that movie," Dad reminisces. He does that lately—reminisces. "Julius did a lot of that kind of thing for me. My parents were always so busy. You know, when I think about it, seeing that movie was probably one of the things that helped convince me to be a minister. Watching a great man who died for his religious beliefs . . ."

"Dad, I have to, uh, go to the bathroom."

He seems distracted now. "Oh, sure, go ahead. I should get back to work anyway." As he picks up the Bible, I notice something sticking out from between the pages. What he must have really been staring at when I walked into the house.

As I start to leave, he says, "Chase?" Struggling. "When I said that about Thomas More . . . dying for his . . . I probably shouldn't have."

"Dad. Don't worry." Wanting to be nice, I add, "It's a good story. I didn't know that movie had such an influence on you."

He smiles. "Okay, then."

I exit the kitchen. In the living room, standing at the mantel, I see the empty space where Dad's picture of him and his brother normally rests. It's been six years since he died. I know Dad really loved him. But there had been two pictures sticking out of the Bible, and I'd like to think the other photo he'd been staring at was the one of Ben that isn't with these others anymore.

Above the display hangs the crucifix, and, as usual, I check it to make sure nothing is broken.

"Is there anything else you feel you have *to do?"* Dr. Braun had asked me in her office.

Nothing is broken.

One-two-three-four. Two-four-six-eight.
Breathe.
Three-six-nine-twelve. Four-eight-twelve-sixteen.
A few more rounds, then I finally go up to my room.

CHAPTER 6

I'm not one to talk much about dreams, but a couple keep coming back. For example:

"Look at me, Chase! I'm Superboy!"

I'm in church, and Dad's preaching the way he used to, and the whole congregation is into it, rocking and swaying. Next to me on the pew my mother has her eyes closed, and she's talking to herself in a low voice as she clutches a Bible to her breasts and sways with the rest of them. And as I lean over to listen, I hear her going, "One-two-three-four, two-four-six-eight," and I realize they're all doing it, the entire congregation, "three-six-nine-twelve, four-eight-twelve-sixteen . . ."

"Look at me, Chase! I'm Superboy!"

It's Ben I hear, and I realize he's not sitting with us. I stand up and find he's not anywhere in the sanctuary. Other people stand now and start to move around the church, still rocking and swaying, making it harder for me to see. As my dad continues to rail from the pulpit, he beckons me forward. But I run the other way, out the door, and find myself outside of the house we lived in when Uncle Julius lived next door.

I look up to the roof, and there's Ben wearing a blanket like a cape and standing near the edge, from where he shouts, "Look at me, Chase! I'm Superboy!"

"What are you doing up there?"

"I'm gonna fly!"

"Ben, oh my God, come down from there," my mother pleads as she runs out of the house with Dad at her side.

"Son, you climb back into the window right now," he orders, referring to the attic window from which my brother must have climbed out. "Right now! Do you hear me?"

"But I can do it, Dad," Ben shouts. "I really can!"

From Mom: "Ben, please . . ."

"I can't be hurt! I'm the boy of steel!"

"Ben, I'm your father, and I'm ordering you . . ."

He spreads the blanket like great wings on a bird . . .

". . . to climb back in that window . . ."

. . . leans forward . . .

". . . right this minute!"

. . . bends his knees . . .

"Noooo!" my mother screams, her cry stretching out into forever, until it sounds like the screeching of brakes. And then sounds like something else.

Angie.

Screaming.

"Quite a dream," Dr. Braun says at our Thursday afternoon session. The whole time I told it, she scribbled madly in her notebook.

"How old was Ben when he jumped off the roof?" she asks.

"Eleven."

"And he broke his arm?'

"Yes."

"What a great dream."

"Why 'great'?" I ask.

"Because there's so much there," she answers, looking at me in surprise. "The church service. Your dad preaching. The congregation swaying like that and counting. Is your dad demonstrative like that behind the pulpit?"

"He used to be," I tell her.

"But not now."

"Not since we moved."

"Which was after Ben went to jail. When your dad left his last church."

"Right."

"At the end of the dream you said your mother's scream turned into the screech of brakes, and then became Angie screaming."

"So?"

"It's all there. Elements of the accident. The church environment you and Ben were raised in. Ben's rebelliousness. Different from you."

"Yeah," I admit hesitantly.

"Dreams are great. They tell us about ourselves, things we hide from our own consciousness. It's interesting that you connect the car accident with something that happened to your brother."

"Why do you say that?"

"Your dream ends with elements of the accident. If we could just figure out what it means—"

"Why do we have to figure it out?"

"Why shouldn't we?"

"It was just a dream."

"Which you said you've had several times."

I shrug.

"Why do *you* think you dream about Ben jumping off the roof when he was eleven?"

"I don't know."

"It must have some significance."

"Why?"

"Come on, let's talk about it."

"I don't want to!"

She stops and does her stare.

"Stop looking at me like that," I tell her. "I don't have to talk about it if I don't want to."

"You're angry."

I look away.

"Didn't you ever talk about dreams in the hospital with Dr. McShane?"

"I didn't have any."

"None at all? In two months?"

"No."

"Actually, we all dream three to six times a night on average. It's just we don't remember most of them."

"So?"

"So you remember this one. Vividly. I wonder why."

I don't have an answer, so I remain quiet.

"You're in a surly mood today," she notes. "Did something happen since I saw you Monday?"

Reluctantly, I start to answer, then shut my mouth.

"Ah, something did," she says, nodding.

"In drama class."

"Really?"

"A couple of things."

"Like what?"

"Well, there was this girl . . ."

"A girl?" She raises an eyebrow.

"Nothing like that," I tell her.

"Nothing like what?"

When I don't respond, she says, "All right. Tell me."

And I do.

Drama is my last class of the day. Russell Hannah, the drama teacher and the guy who directs the two stage productions every year, starts Wednesday's class by announcing, "We're going to pair up for scene work. When I've finished assigning partners and handing out the scenes, spread out and read through them together a few times. You'll have time to practice every day, and in two weeks we'll take a week to present and critique them." He starts calling out names, and when he gets to mine, he says, "Chase, you're with Darla." Darla Prince, the new girl Heather went on about Monday. "Your scene is from *Our Town*, George and Emily, the ice cream soda scene in act two. Start with when they first meet up, when George asks Emily if he can carry her books." He hands us each a copy of the play.

"Who's playing whom?" shouts Roy from his seat, drawing scattered laughter. I glance over at Darla, who seems oblivious to the comment. Dressed in the type of clothes she wears every day. What the kids who talk about her call "butch." She wears no makeup and her hair is almost a buzz cut. Over a heavy build, with wide shoulders and narrow hips, she has on thick wide corduroy pants that are about two sizes too big for her and are hiked high up on her waist, and a heavy flannel shirt even when the weather is mild. The clothes are obviously old and worn and look like items she picked up from a yard sale or the Goodwill store.

"Careful, Roy," Mr. Hannah says. "In Shakespeare's day feminine-looking boys played the women's roles, and I've got parts you'd be perfect for."

That gets a bigger laugh, and Roy gives a "hah-hah" back as he slinks down into his chair. The thing about Roy, when he told his parents he wanted to take drama, his dad asked, "Are you gay?" So he's sensitive about the subject, but while we all joke about it, he's one of the ones who jokes about it the most.

Once we get our assignments, everybody spreads out into the auditorium. Darla puts two seats between us and begins reading the scene to herself, so I do the same, even though I've read the play many times and know the scene.

After only a few minutes Darla mutters, "Yeah, right," and tosses the paperback on the floor.

"What?" I ask.

"Do you really see me playing this part?" She leans over, picks up the book, and reads in a falsetto voice.

"'It's not as easy for a girl to be perfect as a man because we girls are more—more—nervous.' Christ. Mr. Hannah must want me to make an ass out of myself."

"Maybe he just wants to stretch you," I suggest.

"Yeah, I'm sure that's it," she says, frowning and picking up her book bag.

"Why don't we read it through once?"

"Why don't we not and say we did." She drops the book into her bag.

"Hey, this is my assignment too."

"I'll read it at home tonight, then we can go over it tomorrow." She looks at me and sneers. "I promise."

"I don't know . . ."

"Oh, come on, loosen up. You're the stage star of Westfield, I hear. It doesn't matter if you read it or not. You could do it tomorrow, cold."

"Hardly," I mumble. Secretly I'm pleased at the compliment.

"So tell me what it's like."

"What?"

"Being a star."

"Come on." I turn away.

"Hey, help me out. I'm new here. I figure I probably have to get an in somewhere before anyone here will talk to me. You had the lead in the last play, right? I should probably get to know you."

"Hardly."

"Do the same kids get the big parts or what?"

"Are you planning to audition tomorrow?" I ask.

"Probably not."

"Mr. Hannah's pretty fair at giving everyone a chance."

"He hasn't gone out of his way to talk to me."

"I was new here last year and he cast me in *Brigadoon*."

"Yeah, but I'll bet you're talented."

I don't know what to say to that, so I ask, "What kind of theatre did you do in your last school? What plays were you in?"

"Are you kidding? They didn't have a theatre program at my last school. I took this class 'cause I thought it'd be easy." She looks at me. "I guess *you're* going to audition for the big play, though, right?"

"Probably."

"Yeah, right. 'Probably.'"

"Look," I say, irritated, "I don't know what you think of me—"

"You know what I'd really like to know," she interrupts in a low, conspiratorial tone, "is all the theatre dirt. Who's sleeping with whom? Who's gay?"

"I don't know."

"Don't know, or you just aren't gonna tell me."

"Both."

"You must have some idea."

"I don't want to talk about this. Why don't we just read through the scene?"

"Aren't you gonna ask me if I'm gay?"

"Pardon me?"

"You know, a dyke. Because of the way I dress. You must be curious. Everybody else is."

I just shrug my shoulders.

"What, you don't care?"

"It's none of my business."

"Huh. Well." She stares at me, then says, "If you're not gonna ask, I'm not gonna tell you." She glances around the auditorium, and I look with her at the other kids reading their parts, raising their voices and waving their arms.

"Look at them," Darla says sarcastically. "They're all gonna be stars."

As she keeps watching the other kids practice their scenes, I open my copy of the play. I'll read the scene to myself if Darla won't read with me. Maybe even start memorizing my lines.

"You guys finished reading your scene?" I hear Mr. Hannah say. He's leaning over the row in front of us. "Can I talk to you a minute, Chase?"

I glance at Darla, who smiles at both of us. "Go ahead.

I'll have my lines memorized by the time you get back."

We sit in another part of the auditorium. "How are you doing, Chase?" he asks.

"Okay." I like Mr. Hannah. He's not some math or history teacher who just happened to take a drama course somewhere so they made him responsible for directing the two plays every year. He has a degree in theatre and a love for it. He thinks I have the ability for a career if I want. He's also tough. He likes to challenge students. And he's not just interested in doing musicals every year.

"It must be tough coming back here," he says. "I should have come to see you after you were out of the hospital. I'd heard you were home."

"You didn't have to," I say, feeling tense.

"No. I should have. You know, I never told you . . ." He hesitates. "Those first four performances of *Godspell*, you were excellent. A real improvement over what you did in *Brigadoon*. You already had me thinking we should do something more serious this year. A straight play with some meat.

"That Tuesday night we were dark, when I heard what happened. . . . I couldn't believe it. I kept thinking, was there something I missed, something I should have noticed? Giving you the lead in a big play so soon after the accident—in retrospect, I could see you were having a difficult time. Not with learning the part itself—you were doing great. You know how talented I think you are. But dealing with what happened . . . being in the car with those kids who were killed . . . that kind of thing doesn't just go away, I'm sure. I wish I'd been more aware."

"I really don't think there's anything you could have done," I mumble.

"Is there anything I can do now?"

I'm not sure what he's asking. "No, I don't think so."

"To make things easier for you."

"Easier?"

"Tomorrow at the auditions." He leans in. "Look, I know everyone figures you and Kyle are getting the two male leads. I just want things to be as easy for you as possible, Chase. No pressure."

Because he's worried I might hurt myself again if he casts me? Is he really saying he *doesn't* want me to show up tomorrow?

The bell rings, and Mr. Hannah stands up, calling to the class, "Look over your scenes at home. Auditions will start tomorrow at four here in the auditorium."

With his back to me, I hurry away.

"Auditions were today?" Dr. Braun asks in a quiet voice.

I nod.

"We could have rescheduled."

"I decided not to go."

"Why?"

After a moment: "It's better this way. Now he won't have to worry about whether I'll wig out or not."

"Your parents told me you love acting. Isn't that true?"

"Yeah."

"*Are* you afraid you're going to 'wig out' if you do another play?" she asks.

"I don't know. Mr. Hannah's certainly worried about it."

"So this is a big sacrifice you're making. You're being a martyr."

"No."

"I feel humbled in your presence."

"I didn't think therapists were allowed to be sarcastic."

"Where'd you hear that?"

I ignore her.

"I think Mr. Hannah is offering you a chance to play a major role in one of the great plays of American theatre."

"I don't think so."

"I do. He wants to direct the best production, with the best cast he can get. What's wrong with that? You don't think high school drama directors play favorites?"

"I just . . ." I falter, surprised when I have to fight back tears. "I just want people to stop . . ."

"What?"

"Worrying about me. I just want to audition, do my best. . . . I just want things to be . . ."

"Normal," Dr. Braun finishes for me.

I hang my head and wipe my eyes.

"I told you 'normal' was going to be tough. Truth is, I'm not sure it's possible."

"Why not?" Her words make me angry.

"Who defines normal? You want things to be the way they were before? You tried to kill yourself; you can't expect people to treat you the same way they always did. And before that you were in a horrible accident. People you cared for died. You think trying to live your life as if that didn't happen is realistic?"

She pauses. Then asks, "Are you sure you're not doing this to punish yourself?"

"You're the therapist!" I snap. "You tell me!"

"You can cut that out right now."

She roots inside a crushed pack for a cigarette. As she lights it, I say quietly, "You mean, am I punishing myself because of the accident?"

"Are you?" She exhales smoke. "You seem damned set on making the accident your fault."

"But I don't remember. Maybe it *was* my fault."

"Right. Survivor guilt. I lived, therefore I'm to blame."

"Are you making fun of me?"

"No." She leans in. "Listen, I think guilt's a good

thing, especially if you've done something wrong. But in your case, guilt's a waste of time." She pauses again, then sits back. "So tell me what your parents think about your not auditioning."

"I haven't told them yet."

"Where do they think you are right now?"

"Here. I didn't tell them exactly when auditions were."

"You don't tell your parents much, do you?"

"They don't ask."

"They don't?"

"No. They want me to be better, but they don't want to know details."

"You told me Monday that your mom asks about your therapy."

"But it doesn't mean she wants to know. They would both prefer it all just went away."

"Like Ben went away?"

"Yeah," I whisper.

"How did it make you feel to have to move after your brother was sent to jail?"

"I didn't like it, but Dad felt we had to."

"Why?"

The room feels close. Warm. "He couldn't do his job anymore."

"He couldn't?"

"He had to think of his congregation."

"Over his family? His son?"

"I don't think he thought of it like that."

"Well, let me see if I understand. Your brother gets sent to a detention facility that is at least close enough for you to visit him a few times a month, but then your father, two months after Ben goes in, moves you farther away.

"How many times did you visit him, Chase?"

I don't say anything.

"You didn't go see him at all, did you?"

I shake my head. "Did your parents go?"

"Twice," I tell her in a quiet voice. "The first time, a week after he'd gone in. The second time, to tell him about the move."

"But you didn't go either time."

"My dad thought . . ." I hesitate.

"Aren't you pissed off?"

"No."

"Why the hell not? Your parents moved you around a lot, didn't they? That'd make me mad."

"I . . ."

"You didn't like all that moving, right?"

"No."

"Especially the one that took you farther away from Ben."

I shrug.

"You told me you love your brother—"

"Yes. Very much."

"He got taken away from you when he went to jail." She taps the long stem of her ash from her cigarette before it crumbles onto the floor. "Then two months later your dad took you even farther away."

"He couldn't help it."

"You think he did the right thing?"

"I don't know. I didn't want to leave. But it's his job."

"So that makes it okay."

I look at her. "Why are you doing this?"

"I'm just trying to figure out why you aren't willing to get mad at your parents. Don't you feel like screaming at them?"

"Look!" I shout. "This has nothing to do with why I'm here! I thought we were going to talk about why I can't remember the accident."

"Maybe there's a connection."

"What do you mean?"

She waits a minute, staring at me. The old silent game.

"I hate it when you do that."

"Who are you mad at now?" she asks.

"You!" I answer.

"No problem telling *me*, huh? How does it feel?"

"Shitty."

"Fair enough. But do me a favor. Don't be so quick to give up your anger. Hold on to it for a while, even after you leave here. You don't have to do anything with it outside of this office. But when you're here, I want you to feel free to express it. Yell, curse, I don't care. You won't destroy me."

I stay silent. Better to keep quiet for the moment.

"By the way," she says in a quiet voice, "what does Ben say about your not going to auditions?"

"I haven't seen him in a few days."

"Don't you know where he's staying?"

"No."

"You think he'd tell you."

"He has his reasons."

She nods. "Time's about up, but there is one more thing I want to ask. About that memory of Ben when you and he were younger."

"Look at me, Chase! I'm Superboy!"

"What about it?" I ask, nervous.

"Your dream starts with that memory but ends with the car accident. And we know you blame yourself for the latter."

"So?"

"I'm wondering if you also blame yourself for your brother's breaking his arm."

I look at her.

"Do you?"

CHAPTER 7

The sound of pebbles hitting my bedroom window wakes me, and, looking out, I see Ben standing at the side of the house, smiling. "Come down," he calls, motioning.

Outside, the night still feels more like August than September. We sit on the grass in the backyard. "You told me we'd have to find some other place to meet," I remind him.

Ben shrugs. "I wanted to see you. Figured nighttime was easier. Mom and Dad are still sound sleepers, right?"

"Yeah."

"And—I don't know—something told me you might want to talk."

I look at him, but don't say anything. "How were the auditions?" he asks.

After a moment I say, "I didn't go."

"What? Why?"

"I didn't feel like it."

"Aw, come on, Chase. You can act rings around those kids. You know that. What's going on?"

"I just . . . didn't want to this time."

"Bullshit. What is it, are you afraid of messing up again?"

"Maybe."

"Hey, I know about messing up. But here I am. If I can come back, you can too."

"I don't know about that," I say in a low voice.

"You won't mess up."

"How can you be so sure?"

"I believe in you."

"Yeah?"

"You bet. You know that, don't you?"

"It's just . . ." I hesitate, my voice thick with emotion.

Ben waits, but when I don't continue, he glances around in the bright moonlight. "This is a decent backyard. Better than most we've had." Looking at me he says, "Hey, who were those friends we used to get together with and do plays? Remember?"

After a minute I say, "Bobby and Jill Thompson."

"Right," Ben says, nodding. "We had a real big backyard at that house. Would have been nice if we could have stayed there longer. I remember the old lady next door yelled at us 'cause she was afraid we'd go into her yard. How old were you then?"

"Seven," I answer.

"Right. I was nine. What I remember is you loved being the director. Telling everybody what to say, where to stand. Me, I didn't care, so I just let you. Even though you always gave yourself the biggest part. You were a ham bone even then."

"Yeah?" I say. "So what's your point?"

"That you love to freaking act. You like being noticed. And when you're onstage, people notice you. They like you, for God's sake. There's nothing wrong with that. You should have auditioned, Chase."

Above us the night is so clear, the sky so vast, I could get lost up there among the stars.

"Maybe I don't want people to notice me like that anymore," I say. "I could be like everyone else then."

"Why would you want to be like everybody else? That's boring."

When I don't say anything, he asks, "What's bugging you, LB? Come on, you can tell me."

"Remember that time you jumped off the roof and broke your arm?" I ask.

"Why do you keep harping on that?"

"I've been dreaming about it."

"So?"

"I was wondering if you blame me."

"For breaking my arm? What the hell could you have done? Catch me?"

"I'm not . . ." I feel uneasy. Take a deep breath. *One-two-three-four.*

"Chase?" Ben frowns. "What is it?"

"I'm not really talking about you jumping . . ." *Two-four-six-eight.* "I'm talking about . . . what happened . . . you know . . ."

Ben suddenly stands up and walks away. Takes a moment to stare up at the stars. Maybe he's thinking now's a good time for him to leave.

Finally, he turns back. "Yeah, I know what you're talking about. I thought we'd settled that. I thought we weren't going to talk about it." Crouching down, he says, "Listen to me, Chase!" His eyes narrow. "What happened happened. It's been over for how long now? Stop thinking about the past. It doesn't do any good. You did the right thing. Do you hear me?"

"But I—"

"Do you hear me?"

"I should have said something. Things might have been different."

"No. They would have been worse. You know that. So shut up. I don't want to hear about it."

"Maybe you wouldn't have gotten in trouble with the police—"

"Hey! *I* screwed up. Not you. And nothing you say is gonna change that."

I look at him.

"I love you, little brother."

"You do?" I ask. My voice husky.

"Sure. Why do you think I'm still here?"

It's hard to see now, my eyes blurry, despite the clear night and bright moon.

"Let's just sit here for a while," Ben says. "Okay?"

Upstairs, Mom and Dad sleep soundly, unaware their older son is sitting so near.

"Where the hell were you?" Heather says.

"I decided not to audition." I notice one or two kids glancing at us as they pass us in the hall.

"Why? You're only the best actor at Westfield."

"Yeah," I scoff. "So I've heard."

"There'll still be callbacks. I think you should go talk to Mr. Hannah."

"What's the big deal?

"You, me, and Kyle, we'd make this the best production this school's ever done."

"Well, I . . ." I throw up my arms, at a loss for words.

"If this has to do with what you did last spring—"

"Just stop talking about it, Heather! Please!"

She stares a moment, then says in a calmer voice, "Okay. Look, if there's anything else you want to talk about—"

"No."

"You sure?" She puts a hand softly on my arm. It makes me flinch.

She smiles, hurt, and says, "Well, you know where to find me."

She walks away. And even though I don't want to, I can't help but remember that afternoon last year, after school, in the auditorium. Angie standing at the entrance, a look of horror on her face. Heather pulling herself out from under me in the auditorium seat, clothes disheveled, face flushed, eyes wide, and maybe looking pleased with herself as Angie turns to leave. By the time I disentangle myself and race out into the hall, she's gone, and it isn't until the next day that I get a chance to talk to her, to explain, though without an excuse, what can I do but tell her how sorry I am? *I'm sorry, Angie. Can you forgive me? I love you—*

The bell interrupts my thoughts. The hall is almost empty, and the few stragglers seem to be looking at me. Who needs to audition for the school play? I'm onstage anyway.

Eighth period arrives and, walking into the auditorium, I make a beeline for the seat next to Darla, who's sitting off by herself, as usual. Mr. Hannah stares at me. "All right, everybody," he says to the class, "work on your scenes."

"When's the callback list going up?" Kyle asks.

"Monday morning, like I said," he answers. "Do your scene work."

Darla follows me as I go far back in the auditorium and yank out my copy of *Our Town*. Her outfit is a different color flannel shirt and corduroy pants, and as she sits next to me, she lifts her book bag. "Are we finally going to read the scene today?" I ask. She forgot to bring her copy of the play yesterday so we didn't get to practice.

"I forgot it again."

"What?"

"I had it sitting out in my room and I just didn't pick it up." She shrugs. "What can I say?"

"Great," I mumble.

"You take this seriously, don't you?"

"I just want . . . never mind."

"How about we just talk?"

After a moment I say, "What about?"

"Hey, I'm new here, remember? I'm still waiting to hear the dirt. Not too many people seem to want to talk to me."

"Do you want them to?" I say without thinking.

She looks at me. "What's that supposed to mean?"

"Nothing. Forget it."

"Oh, I see. 'Cause of the way I dress. And wear my hair. You figure I do it so people will stay away."

I glance at her, look away. Then turn back. "Or make people notice."

"And your point is?"

How did I get into this? "Nothing. I'm sorry. I'm just in a bad mood today."

"What about?"

"Nothing. I . . . I'm just gonna read the scene to myself, okay?"

I open the book, but before I get to the bottom of the page, I hear Darla say, "I learned something about you I didn't know."

"Yeah?" I respond without looking up. "What's that?"

"You're the kid who tried to kill himself."

I look up.

"Now that's a way to get noticed," she says with a smile.

I stare. "How did you . . . ? I thought you said kids here don't talk to you."

"It doesn't mean I don't eavesdrop on them." Darla leans in, eyes wide, and says, "Tell me about it."

"Why?"

"I'm curious. I don't know anybody who's ever tried suicide. Did it hurt? Or didn't you feel anything?"

I turn away.

"Just tell me why you chose to cut your wrists. It takes a long time to bleed, doesn't it? Is that why you chose it?"

"Please . . ."

"I read once the method a suicidal person chooses says a lot about him. Sleeping pills, that's simple. But somebody has to really be pissed to jump off a building or hang themselves . . ."

I look at her.

". . . or crash a car . . ."

Suddenly . . .

I'm flying. Then I hit pavement.

Then I'm back in my auditorium seat, out of breath.

"Do you mind showing me the scars?" I hear Darla ask.

"What?"

"On your wrists. I really am curious."

Again. *I'm flying. Then I hit pavement.*

"Why aren't you two practicing your scene?"

Mr. Hannah asks, coming toward us, and the flash of memory is gone.

Darla raises her hand. "My fault," she responds, smirking. "I left my copy at home."

"I remembered you forgot it yesterday, so I brought another one just in case." My drama teacher pulls a book from his back pocket. "I'll be glad to let you borrow it.

"Is there a problem?" he asks when she doesn't take it.

"I don't think this part's for me," she answers.

"Well, you can give it a try, can't you?"

"I'd rather have another part."

"I decide the parts, and I assigned you this one."

He keeps his hand extended, and eventually she takes the book. Then Mr. Hannah folds his arms and remains that way until Darla asks, "What are you doing?"

"I'm waiting for you two to get started."

I can see Darla's neck starting to turn red. "Mr. Hannah?" I say.

"Yes, Chase?"

Surprised by his coldness, I just ask, "Where do you want us to start?"

"Start with George's line, 'Emily, why are you mad at me?'"

"What about the lines the stage manager has?"

"I'll do those. In fact, I'll tell you what, in a couple of weeks when you perform this, I'll do the stage manager's lines from offstage. Take the scene to the end, when the two of them leave the soda shop. Don't worry, I know my lines."

I've never seen him this way. I glance at Darla. I can't describe the look on her face. The red in her neck has turned almost purple, and the color is creeping up her face. She hasn't moved. Not a muscle. She stares at Mr. Hannah without even blinking.

"Go ahead, Chase," he says.

I look down and begin. "'Emily, why are you mad at me?'"

Darla reads back to me in a dry, deep monotone, "'I'm not mad at you.'"

"'You've been treating me so funny lately.'"

"You can do better than that, Chase."

I look up at Mr. Hannah, mouth open. "I'm just reading—"

"I can tell. Put a little more feeling into it."

I pause, then repeat my last line. "'You've been treating me so funny lately.'"

"'Well,'" Darla reads again in monotone, "'since you ask me, I might as well say it right out, George—'"

"How about you put a little more feeling into it too, Darla?" Mr. Hannah says.

"She's reading it out loud for the first time," I say.

"That doesn't mean—"

"This sucks," she says in her same dead Emily voice.

Mr. Hannah's eyes widen. "Maybe," he tells her. "But I still think you should give it a try."

Darla stands. "I don't have to try anything I don't want to," she announces, and, dropping the book, she walks out of the auditorium.

A few of the other kids stare and begin muttering to each other. When someone starts to laugh, Mr. Hannah orders, "Everybody get back to work!"

I see Heather mouth to me, "Meet me after class."

To me Mr. Hannah says, "I'm sorry about that. I don't know what's wrong. Are you two getting along?"

"She was just nervous."

"Maybe." Mr. Hannah shakes his head. "But it doesn't mean she can just walk out."

"Why did you give her that role?" I hear myself ask. The voice coming out of me seems different. More like Ben's, maybe, because he's the kind that questions people. Not me. "The part of Emily couldn't be more different from who she is. I think she was embarrassed. It's her first time. You could have given her something easier." *Is that what he wanted?* I ask myself. *To make it difficult for her?*

"Why don't we talk over here."

He turns, and I follow him halfheartedly. "I don't know if your not showing up yesterday means you don't want to be in the play," he says over his shoulder, "but I'd like you to reconsider. It's a great opportunity for someone with your talent. I'd really like to give you the chance. . . ." Reaching his briefcase near the front of the auditorium entrance, he bends down to open it.

"Come here, Chase, I've got something to show you."

"Come here, Chase, I've got something to show you."

"Right here I've got . . ." Looking at me, Mr. Hannah straightens, then frowns. "What is it?"

In my mind's eye I see the figure of Jesus on the cross. Those suffering eyes staring right into me.

And I hear *"Come here, Chase, I've got something to show you."*

"Chase?"

"Come here—"

"Is something wrong?"

"What?" I mumble, the image gone.

"I said is there something—"

"No!" I cut him off. Tense, heart thumping. "Nothing." *One-two-three-four. Two-four-six-eight.* Breathe. "What were you saying before?"

"I've got copies of *A Man for All Seasons*. Why don't you do an audition for me now?"

"I don't want to be in the play, Mr. Hannah."

He stares at me, and I feel guilty. Abruptly he says, "If that's what you want. Do you have any homework you can do for the rest of the period?" Without waiting for an answer, he picks up his briefcase and starts to walk away. Stops. Looks back at me.

"Chase . . . are you okay?"

"Yes," I say, turning to go back to my seat. "Sure."

CHAPTER 8

Saturday's the one morning my parents don't wake me up. Dad has church office hours, and Mom's either at one of her committee meetings or visiting church members. She loves being seen. She won't let having a son just out of the mental ward slow her down.

I've been lying here thinking.

I wish Ben were here. I need to talk to him. But what if he came by and Mom or Dad showed up without warning? He's got his own life now that he's out of jail. How much longer can I expect him to stay just for me?

I see my brother standing on the roof when he was eleven. Always taking risks to make Mom and Dad notice.

"Son, you climb back into the window right now. Right now!"

His broken arm took four weeks to heal. But then he was back to his normal self.

"I can't be hurt! I'm the boy of steel!"

Indestructible.

I glance at the clock. It's almost eleven. I hear nothing. Not even a creak. Mom hasn't returned. Dad usually stays at his office until noon.

The phone rings.

I pick up the receiver. "Hello?"

"Where were you?" Heather.

"Pardon?"

"Yesterday after school. I told you to meet me."

Thinking fast I say, "You didn't say where."

"My locker, where else?"

"Heather, you caught me just getting up."

"You're still in bed? Maybe I should come right over."

"What do you want?"

Silence. Did I hurt her feelings? "I want to know what happened in drama yesterday," she says. "Why Darla walked out?"

"She didn't like the scene Mr. Hannah assigned her."

"She'd never play Emily if she were a professional. She couldn't even play George."

"I think what he did was unfair."

"Unfair?"

"He should have chosen a role more like her."

"There aren't any plays about Godzilla."

"Heather—"

"Come on, look at her," she interrupts. "She's a total dyke."

I don't respond.

"Hey, are you okay?" she asks.

"Yeah."

"You haven't taken me up on my offer."

"Offer?"

"To talk."

"There's nothing to talk about," I say.

"What did Mr. Hannah say to you in his office?"

"He offered to let me audition."

"Why didn't you?"

"Why does anybody care whether I do or not?"

"I want you in the play 'cause you're the best damn actor in Westfield," Heather says. "You'll make the play good. You'll make *me* look good. I'm not too proud to say it."

I say nothing.

"I don't know if you heard," she continues, "but Principal Jarvis didn't want us doing *A Man for All Seasons*. He wants musicals all the time 'cause they make lots of money for the school. Mr. Hannah really had to talk him into it, convince him it would be great because of the kids he had this year. You especially, Chase, whether you want to believe it or not. *Godspell*'s opening night went so well, Mr. Jarvis gave in and wrote the check for the rights the next day."

Before I pulled my razor trick.

"I hear Mr. Jarvis isn't sure he did the right thing anymore. Mr. Hannah wants to prove him wrong."

"Do it!" I remember the voice saying.

"You there?"

"Huh?" I grunt.

"Jeez, you're acting spacey. If you're not gonna audition, you gonna do stage crew?"

"Maybe," I say, head spinning.

"I guess you won't be going to Kyle's party next Saturday. It'll just be for the cast."

"I . . . I guess not."

"You can damn well bet *I'm* gonna be in the show. I'm called back for the part of Margaret, Thomas More's daughter. Mr. Hannah told me."

"Hope you get it."

The heavy silence on the other end feels like an indictment.

"Look," I say, "it's a quarter after eleven. I gotta—"

"I know why you're really avoiding me."

"What?" I ask, confused.

"I'm sorry too," Heather says. "Sorry she saw us. Sorry you two broke up because of me." In a softer voice, "I'm sorry she's gone. At the memorial service that's all I could think about. I didn't know the others, even though Dan was in *Brigadoon*."

"Maybe we shouldn't see each other for a while, Chase," I remember Angie saying in a sad voice the morning after she'd found me with Heather. I'd telephoned her the night before, but she'd refused to take my call.

"I'm sorry, Angie. I made a mistake."

"Yes." She nods. "You did."

"What can I do?" I beg. "Please tell me."

"Nothing, Chase. I need time."

"How much time?"

"I don't know." She manages a sad smile. "You're not losing me," she says. "I'm still your friend."

"Yeah?" I whisper.

She touches my cheek. "Always."

After a while she started dating Kevin Harris.

"You there?" Heather.

"I'm here." Clutching the phone.

"I've gotta go. Think about what I said. About talking."

"Okay."

"Bye, Chase."

"Good—" I hear the click breaking the connection. But I still hear a voice on the other end.

"Do you need me to come get you, Chase?"

Angie's voice.

Another memory from the party.

"If you don't mind." My voice. *"I'm afraid we're all—"*

"Drunk?"

"Yeah." I hear Dan's drunken laugh. He must have been right next to me.

"I'm on my way," Angie says.

"No!" I shout into the phone. "Don't come, Angie! Stay home. We'll find another way—"

The dial tone cuts in.

"Chase?"

Coming up the stairs. My father. Home early.

"Are you in there?"

The dial tone stops, followed by that recording, *"If you'd like to place a call . . ."*

A knock on the door. "Can I come in?"

"Uh . . . sure."

The door swings open. He's tall, my dad. Six-four. Gangly. He played on his high school basketball team. But he walks around hunched over. I remember how tall he used to stand during his sermons.

"Everything okay, Chase? I thought I heard you—"

"I'm fine. I was—"

"—yelling."

"—on the phone. Pardon?"

"Excuse me?"

"You said something."

"I heard you yelling."

"No. I was on the phone."

"Oh." We both let out a deep breath. "I tried calling," Dad says, "to let you know I was coming home early. But, of course . . . you were on the phone."

"Yeah."

He smiles. I'd forgotten how good a smile looks on him.

"Who with?"

"What?" I ask.

He indicates the phone in my hand. "Who called?"

I put back the receiver. "Heather."

"She's in your drama group, right? You should have her over sometime. Your other friends from drama group too."

"Okay." Silence. Dad shuffles his feet, his hands in his pockets.

"I thought we could do something."

"Yeah?"

"We haven't done anything in a long time. Just the two of us. You just now getting up?

"Uh-huh."

"Are you feeling okay?"

I nod.

"Good. When I was a teenager, I used to sleep late

on Saturdays. Hey, you think there's time to get down to the ballpark to see the game?"

"They're not home this weekend," I say, though I don't know the Phillies' schedule.

"How about a movie, then? There's probably something good at the AMC—"

"I don't feel like a movie today, Dad."

"This is my son talking?"

I look down at the floor, then back up. "How's your sermon coming?"

"It's coming."

"It's hard work? Writing a sermon?"

"Sometimes." He hesitates. "You seem . . . a little better, Chase."

Surprised, I don't know what to say.

"Our youth group has a meeting tomorrow. If you're interested in going . . ." Again, he hesitates. "This is a nice church. Nice people. People we can settle in with, I think . . ."

"I don't know if I can go," I say.

"It's up to you. I'm sure you're busy with school." He shakes his head. "Gosh, what am I thinking? You've got the play coming up. How did auditions go?"

"All right," I answer after a moment.

"Hear anything about what part you got?"

"Callbacks are on Monday."

"What do you say in the theatre? Break a leg." He chuckles. "Want some lunch? Or in your case, breakfast? We'll talk."

"About what?"

"Anything you want. You are going to change, right? You're not planning to wear pajamas all day."

I grin sheepishly. "I'll be down in a minute."

He turns toward the hall. "Eggs?"

"Sure."

"Scrambled okay? Heck, how about some sausage, too?"

It doesn't take too long to get past the mantel while Dad's cooking in the kitchen. At the table Dad doesn't say, "Are you okay?" He asks me about the fall movies coming out soon and which ones are potential Oscar material. I haven't paid attention lately.

"Well, then, you've got catching up to do," He laughs, and I laugh too, and after we're finished eating, we don't know Mom has come into the kitchen until Dad starts to get up for more coffee and sees her. "Mary Beth. How was your meeting?"

She looks at me with a cold, hard expression I only started seeing after Ben went to prison. And, suddenly, everything good from the last half hour gets shot away like a giant rubber band snapping my insides.

"Mary Beth?" Dad says, rising. "What's wrong?"

"We need to talk with our son," she says in a hushed voice.

"About what?" Dad glances at me.

"About what I found out at Alice Mayfield's today." She stares at me. "Kyle's mother. I was telling her Chase and Kyle were sure to get the main roles. And she informed me that Chase wasn't at the auditions."

Dad turns. "Chase? You didn't go to the auditions?"

"No," I mutter.

"Are you going to the callbacks? Surely Mr. Hannah—"

"No." I hang my head.

"Why? It's *A Man for All Seasons*. A great play."

"Where were you during the auditions?" Mom asks.

"At my appointment with Dr. Braun," I mumble.

"She wouldn't let you out of one appointment to go to auditions?" Dad says.

"She didn't know about them."

"I asked you how the auditions went. You said they went fine."

"But I didn't say I was there."

"Do you remember, Matt? It started like this with—" She almost says Ben's name. But she catches herself and turns away, blinking back tears.

Say it! I want to shout. *You never say his name. Ben! He's back, and you don't know it. He's come to see me. Not you. Me!*

But I promised I wouldn't tell them. I promised!

Dad takes a deep breath. "It's okay if you don't want to audition. Right, Mary Beth?" She looks at him, then at me, then finally nods. "I just don't understand why you felt you couldn't tell us, Chase."

I should probably say something, but I don't.

"Is it because . . . of what happened last year? During *Godspell*?"

This is the first time Dad or Mom has tried to talk to me about it.

"I couldn't . . ." I can't get the words to form.

"I'm sure everyone understands—"

"No, they don't, Dad. Everybody thinks I'm a freak."

"Surely they don't think that."

"They do!" I almost shout.

But the phone rings.

Staring at me, Dad walks slowly over to answer it. "Hello. Reverend Farrell." After listening a moment, he says, "Okay, Joan. I'll meet you there." Putting the receiver down, he says to Mom, "That was Joan Munro. Her mother collapsed, and she's being taken to the hospital."

"I'll go with you," Mom says.

"You don't have to—"

"You know how fragile Joan is when it comes to her mother. You're going to need a woman's touch."

"Okay. You've got a point." Turning to me he asks, "Are we okay now, Chase?"

I just nod.

"I don't know how long this will take," he informs me in his official pastor voice.

"There are leftovers in the fridge if we're not back by dinner," Mom adds, in official pastor's spouse mode.

"If we're going to be very late, we'll call," Dad finishes, and off they go to jump atop their white steeds and ride to the rescue.

Leaving me standing in the kitchen. Unable to move.

One-two-three-four. Two-four-six-eight. Breathe. *Three-six-nine-twelve. Four-eight-twelve-sixteen.*

I don't know how much time passes before I begin to feel better and head up to my room. Stopping at the mantel first. The figure hanging. The eyes terrible. I stop, check. Nothing's changed. Count. *One-two-three-four.* Up to sixteen. Check again. Start over. Nine, ten times I go through it. If it got broken, Dad would be so upset.

Finally, I head up the stairs.

Looking out my window, I think of Ben. It's only been a few days since I last saw him, but it feels longer. Where is he? Maybe he's been watching from a distance, where I can't see him, waiting for our parents to leave so he can come in.

I wait. He doesn't come.

Maybe he's left town. No, he wouldn't leave without telling me first.

I stare out the window for a long time, as if by doing so I can make him appear out of thin air.

And the day passes slowly.

CHAPTER 9

"After the phone call, they just left you there?" Dr. Braun says.

"That's a minister's life. Someone needs help, you drop everything and go."

"Did your mom have to?"

"She's his helper. She likes doing it."

"So being a minister comes before everything else. Including family."

"I guess."

"Doesn't that piss you off?"

I shrug. "It comes with the territory."

"Maybe your mom understands that because she chose that life. But you didn't. You were born into it. You didn't have a choice."

I keep quiet.

"It must feel like it takes a life or death situation to get their attention."

"You saying I sliced my wrists to get their attention?"

"Did you?"

"I wasn't planning on living, so I guess not."

"Ben must have really been pissed to do the dangerous stuff he did," she says.

"Maybe."

"Did you ever feel that angry at your Mom and Dad?"

"No."

"Why not?"

"They were always upset with him. They didn't need to hear it from me, too."

"So you did get mad. You just didn't tell them."

"That's not what I meant."

"Why didn't you tell your parents about skipping auditions?"

"I don't know." I begin wondering how much time is left in the session. "I just didn't tell them."

"How did you think they'd react when they found out?"

"I didn't."

"Sure you did."

"What?"

"You had a pretty good idea how they'd act," she says. "I doubt it came as a surprise."

"You think I did it on purpose?"

"Did you?"

"No . . . but I guess you think different."

"You could have just told them you wanted time to do other things. They would have understood."

"No."

"Really? Your dad suggested getting involved in youth group."

"He didn't mean it."

"Why do you say that?"

"He expects things of me. They both do."

"They *expect* you to be in the school play?"

"I've been in school plays since middle school."

"They force you to audition?"

"No."

"But they're proud of you when you're onstage."

"They can point and say, 'There's our son. *Our* son.'"

She pauses. "Are you saying it becomes more about them than you?"

"Yeah, maybe."

"Or are you saying the only time they really pay attention to you is when you're onstage?"

I stare at her.

"Seems to me, by not telling them, you got what you wanted."

"What I wanted?"

"What better way to get back at them than by *not* telling them and seeing their reactions when they find out?"

"I still don't understand."

"You forced them to pay attention to you. And, for a while, they did, at least until that phone call."

I say nothing. Look away.

"Obviously they're not perfect parents, Chase. But my point is, you play the game too. Wholeheartedly, I might add.

"Try being direct. I know that scares you, so try it here first."

She reaches for a cigarette. For once she didn't start the session by smoking. "I was thinking about trying to quit, but the hell with it. It's a filthy habit—I know."

After lighting it and opening the window, she points the bright orange end at me. "You keep too many secrets."

"What?"

"I'm not sure why. It's how you deal with your parents, and life. Hell, you do it to yourself."

"Myself?"

"You're keeping at least one big secret from yourself. The accident."

"It's coming back. Like Dr. McShane said it would."

"But you use secrets to get control. For example, nobody else but me knows about your counting, right? And I had to pry it out of you. I imagine there are other rituals you haven't told me about."

I keep quiet.

"Ben sought control by being dangerous. And got all the attention growing up. It didn't leave much for you. Before you tried suicide, your parents probably thought they didn't have to worry about you. You were the good kid."

"I'm not—" I stop.

"What?" she asks. "Not good?"

"I remembered something else."

You're trying to change the subject, her expression says. But she still asks, "Really? What?"

I tell her about the memory of flying, then hitting pavement.

"So now you remember falling out of the car," Dr. Braun says as she taps the long gray ash into her palm and dumps it into the ashtray.

"I guess."

"You were lucky. You could have been hurt bad."

I tell her about remembering the phone conversation with Angie at the party.

"So you called her."

"Yes."

"You do know that does not mean the accident was your fault."

I say nothing.

"Chase?"

"You keep telling me that."

"She could have said no."

"I could have not gotten drunk that night."

"At least you did the responsible thing."

"Responsible?"

"I'm not condoning teenage drinking. But instead of getting behind the wheel plastered, you called somebody to take you home. That's more than that rotten bastard who hit you did. His blood alcohol level was off the charts. You want to blame somebody, you should blame him."

"He's dead."

"So? Don't you hope he's rotting in hell?"

"Maybe," I say. But I'm thinking, *If I hadn't gotten drunk, hadn't called her, hadn't even* gone *to the damn party . . .*

"By the way," Dr. Braun says, "I'm proud of you."

"Huh?"

"For defending that girl in drama class. It wasn't fair of your teacher to give her that part."

"Thanks. I guess." I'm reminded of one other new memory.

"Come here, I've got something to show you."

But I keep it to myself.

"Oh, you're so freaking modest, I can't stand it."

"Mr. Hannah—"

"Disappointed you?"

After a moment I nod in agreement. "It was like he wanted Darla to fail."

"Why do you think he'd want that?"

"Because . . . she's not like the rest of the theatre group."

Dr. Braun drops off another long trail of ash. "I think one of the shittiest things about being a teenager is finding out that your parents and other adults you've looked up to for so long have clay feet."

Silence.

"Was there something else you wanted to tell me?"

Actually, yes.

At school today things are going better. People aren't staring as much.

Darla is still in drama, and I sit next to her.

"Are you surprised to see me?" she says with a smirk.

"Yeah." I'm pleased she's here. "I thought maybe—"

"I quit? Nah." She grins.

"Why?"

"I like hanging out with you."

"Really?"

"Really. Hey!"

"What?"

"You're smiling, Farrell."

I guess I am.

Mr. Hannah comes over. "Here," he says, handing us each a book. "I'm giving you a new assignment. The opening scene from *Death of a Salesman*. Willy and Linda Loman. They're older characters, but it's a classic scene. I'd like to see what you do with it, Chase." He turns and walks away.

"Do I look older?" Darla asks.

"Do I?"

"Definitely," she says. We both laugh.

"It's a good part," I assure her.

"Good." She grins. "Let's read."

It goes well.

"Hey, you walk home, right?" Darla asks me in the hall.

"Right."

"I'll walk with you."

That surprises me. "I don't know . . ."

"You don't want people to see us together?"

"No, it's not . . . Where do you live?"

"Let me get my stuff."

She hurries off. Her locker's far enough away, I can

just leave and explain tomorrow that I like to walk by myself so I can be alone with my thoughts.

Better to tell her that than tell her I'm not going home because I have to go to therapy.

I leave through one of the side exits. Head out past the back of the school.

"Hey, Chase, wait up."

I turn, and here comes Kevin Harris with his two goons.

I pick up my pace. Then feel a rough hand on my shoulder. "Hey! I told you to wait up."

"I . . . I'm sorry, Kevin. I gotta get going."

Fall weather still hasn't kicked in, so the three of them are wearing T-shirts that show off their muscles.

"Take a breath, Farrell," Kevin says. "Do you really have to go? I thought I'd buy you that burger I promised."

"Your friends, too?"

"Nah. Just you and me."

"Watch it, Kevin," Mitch says. "You never know with these theatre faggots."

"Shut up!" Back to me. "Ignore him. He's just kidding around."

"I wish I had something to tell you, Kevin."

"I don't think he wants to tell you," Lars says.

"You know, Farrell," Kevin says, "I'm not some dumb jock. I've got feelings." In a quieter voice, "I know this isn't easy for you. But what happened . . . tore me up too. The guy going eighty-five miles an hour. It must have . . . But somehow you survived, even though you were next to her in the front seat. You were there for Angie's last moments. And I wasn't." His voice chokes, and Lars and Mitch seem embarrassed, and glare at me.

"I fell out of the car," I whisper.

Kevin leans closer. "I know it sounds stupid to say this, but maybe if I had been there, I could have done something. I was supposed to go out with her that night. But the team planned this big get-together at the last minute, and I'm one of the captains so I had to go. Angie understood."

His grip tightens. "You called her late, so chances are she would have been home anyway, but I think about how, if I'd gone out with her like we'd planned, things might have been different."

"I don't know what you want from me, Kevin."

"Or maybe I would have been with her when you called, and if I'd been in the car, I could have done something. Do you know why she didn't see the other car? If he was going eighty-five miles an hour, Jesus, there probably wasn't any time. . . . Was that what happened? There just wasn't enough time?"

Laughter.

"Farrell?"

"I'm sorry—"

Suddenly I see her.

"What is it, Farrell?"

Angie. Looking at me a split second before the collision. Sheer anguish on her face. And I realize that she knew.

"Do you remember something?"

Oh, God, she knew!

"I fell out," I tell him.

"You said that already. It was in the newspaper."

She knew. It's almost too much to bear.

"Farrell?"

Too much.

"Farrell!"

"Is he freaking out again?" Lars.

"Farrell, are you okay?"

"I'm fine," I tell Kevin. Feeling like I might throw up. "I've gotta go."

Kevin grabs me again. "Don't. We can still—"

"Let go of me."

"Tell me what you just remembered."

"I think I'm going to be sick."

"What the hell are you hiding?"

"I'm not—"

"You know what I think?" Kevin says in a drastically different tone. "I think you tried to put the make on her and that's why you don't want to tell me. You were drunk, and figured since you used to go out with her you could get a cheap feel. Forgetting the fact you were in a moving car."

"No." His friends start toward me. "That didn't happen."

"How do you know? You claim you don't remember." They begin to crowd me, and I have no place to go. "Maybe she had to push you away and that's why she didn't see the car coming—"

"Well, there you are." Darla. "I thought you'd left without me."

Putting herself between the wrestlers and me, she says, "I'm ready if you are, Chase."

"You've got it wrong, uh, what's your name . . . Darla?" Kevin tries smiling. "Chase and I are going out."

"Oh, I don't think he's your type," she says, smiling back.

Lars steps forward. "What do you mean by that?"

"On the other hand this guy looks very much your type. I'll bet you two would make quite a pair in your cute little wrestling tights."

"Shut up, dyke!"

"Wow. Dyke. I never hear that one."

The two move closer, but Kevin puts out his hand. "I'm not interested in a fight. I'm just . . ." To Darla he says, "You'll have to do this another time."

"No, I think you and your muscle-head buddies should just go away."

Darla urges me to get moving. But my insides feel like lead.

"You're not going anywhere," I hear Kevin say.

"Who's gonna stop us?" Darla.

"We are." Mitch.

"Really?" Darla.

Lars. "You think just because you're a girl—"

"I think I can kick the crap out of both of you. Shall we see?" To Lars. "Come on, asshole. Show me what you got."

Mitch growls, "Let's get 'em both, Lars."

"Stop!" Kevin orders.

Mitch doesn't react. Darla, to her credit, doesn't budge.

"I said stop! I mean it!" Putting his hand on Mitch's arm, Kevin says, "Let's get out of here."

"You better watch yourself, lesbo—"

"Shut up, Lars. Let's go." Turning back to me, Kevin adds, "But don't think for a minute—"

"She knew!" I blurt out. And suddenly I can't stop. "I remember her face. Her eyes. She knew she was going to die." I'm crying and I don't care. "You want me to say it happened fast, she didn't suffer? But she did.

She knew she was about to die and there was nothing she could do about it. Nothing.

"Do you feel better now?" I ask.

We stand in silence for a long time.

"I'm sorry," I tell him. "I shouldn't have—"

He puts up his hand, then motions to his friends, and they walk away.

Darla takes my hand and says in a gentle voice, "Let's go."

After walking awhile in silence I whisper, "If you want, I'll show you."

"Show me what?" she asks.

"I was thinking about what you asked me the other day. I'll show you my scars. If you still want to see them."

She stops to look at me, and nods. Slowly I roll up my sleeves so she can see the insides of my arms. "I did a sloppy job."

She holds my arms and stares at the wounds the way my father does when holding the Eucharist and cup on Sunday mornings. Then, just as solemnly, she pulls each of my sleeves down until the scars are, again, hidden from view.

"Why did you do it?"

"I don't know," I tell her.

Gently she leads me to a nearby bench. "Tell me whatever you can."

"Why do you want to know?"

"Let's just say . . . I've thought about it myself. Though I wouldn't have the guts. Sometimes I wonder . . . What if I wasn't here anymore? Just . . . gone." She takes a deep breath. "I get freaky thoughts like that sometimes."

She waits until I'm looking at her before she asks, "Do you remember what you were feeling right before you did it?"

I think about it. "No. It wasn't something I'd been planning. It just . . . happened."

"Were you nervous?"

"Sure."

"What else?"

"Somebody told me recently that we all dream several dreams a night but don't remember most of them," I say. "One I do remember . . . Have you ever heard of the actor's nightmare?"

"You're onstage naked and can't remember your lines?"

I smile. "My version's different. The curtain has just come down. I'm waiting in the dark to do the curtain call. But nothing's happening. I don't know what to do. I have to be in position. But what if the curtain never moves? And if I leave and it does go up and I'm not there . . . what then? I'm trapped."

I look at her. "Sounds stupid, doesn't it?"

"Actually, no."

The unseasonably warm air doesn't seem so oppressive now. There's even a breeze, suggesting maybe real fall weather is not that far away.

"Thank you for answering my questions," Darla says.

"I didn't like you asking me about it in drama. But I realized most people just talk around it. Or they act like it'll go away if I just eat the right food or get cast in a good play. My parents ask how I'm doing, but don't talk about *what* I did. They don't ask how I feel about it or say how they feel. I figured that was okay. After a while things would return to normal. But now I know that that's impossible."

"What the hell is normal anyway?" Darla scoffs. "I hate normal."

"Really?"

"Why do you think I dress the way I do?"

We both laugh. "What do your mom and dad think about your clothes?" I ask.

"Mom thinks it's a phase." She grins. "Actually, she's kind of cool. When she was a teenager, she was wild. Even admits she did drugs, which I've never tried, by the way. Of course, that doesn't mean there aren't a few things I wish I hadn't done."

When she doesn't elaborate, I ask, "Like what?"

"Like, I don't want to tell you."

"What's your dad like?"

"He travels a lot in his job. His job is why I'm the new kid in school a lot. His bosses like to send him to a new office every year or two. But he still ends up on the road all the time."

"We've moved around a lot," I tell her. "My dad's a minister, and he used to do a lot of filling in for churches that needed temporary pastors."

"It sucks, doesn't it?" Darla says. "Did your mom give your dad a hard time about it?"

"Are you kidding? My mother loves being a pastor's wife."

"My parents have had rough patches. But they're hanging in there. Mom especially. She's tough."

Silence. Then, out of the blue, Darla says, "The girl that guy Kevin was talking about. Angie. Did you love her?"

After a moment, "Yes."

"Didn't she know how you felt?"

"She knew. We broke up after going out for four months. I was the new kid in school, and for some reason she liked me."

"You're not bad-looking."

"Thanks."

"Why'd you break up?"

Butterflies come alive in my stomach. "I blew it. She found me with somebody. A girl from drama class."

"Heather?"

I nod. "How'd you guess?"

"The way she looks at you."

"Heather kept coming on to me. I ignored her, but she could be pushy. And she's hot." I glance at Darla and keep talking. "One day, after school, Heather and I had a scene to do for class. We practiced in the auditorium. She came on to me again, and I . . . gave in. Angie walked in on us. Later, she said she needed time, but I think she was just letting me down slowly. After a while, she started dating Kevin."

"A theatre geek then a wrestling jock," Darla says. "She sure had varied tastes. So, did Heather go out with you after that?"

"No."

"Bitch."

"I think she felt bad."

"I doubt it."

"She's a friend."

"Some friend."

"You don't know her."

"Oh, yes I do. Girls like that—"

"I guess you're perfect then."

She looks at me. "Why are you defending her?"

I hesitate. "I don't know."

"Girl like that," she says, "she wants attention. It's all about her. You weren't giving her enough attention, so she made sure you did."

"But why?"

"Who knows? New kid, very talented, but you were dating somebody not part of the group. Or maybe she just wanted to see if she could do it." Darla shakes her head. "So what do you think Angie saw in Kevin?"

"I don't know."

"There's a lot you don't know."

"What do you mean?" I ask, puzzled.

"You don't know why Angie liked you, why you cheated on her with Heather. Why she decided to go out with Kevin. Do you just take whatever life dumps on you?"

It's better not to say anything.

"Have you been seeing a shrink?"

I nod. "She thinks my not remembering . . . has to do with more than just the accident."

"What does that mean?"

Warning bells sound in my head. "I don't know."

She stares.

"I don't. Really."

"How often do you go?" Darla asks.

"Twice a week. Mondays and Thursdays."

"You have an appointment today?"

"Her office is just a couple blocks from here."

"And here I thought we were walking to your house."

I say nothing.

"Is there anybody else you talk to?"

Should I tell her? Why not? "My brother. Ben."

"You have a brother? Is he older or younger?"

"Two years older."

"Did he go to school here?"

"No. My parents and I moved here a little over a year ago."

"Oh, that's right. Is he in college?"

"No. He's been in youth detention. He just got out, actually."

"What'd he do?"

I haven't told anybody, and I'm not sure why I decide to tell Darla.

"He and some guys robbed this old man. The guy resisted, and it got out of hand. Ben went crazy. Beat the old man up. Bad. It was supposed to be a simple robbery."

"Look at me, Chase! I'm Superboy!"

"How old was he?"

"I'm gonna fly!"

"Eleven."

"I thought you said he was older."

"Sorry. I was thinking of something else."

"Something else?"

"I'm sorry."

"You're sweating like a pig."

"I'm okay. He was seventeen."

"You're sixteen, right? So he's eighteen now. Wow, he lucked out. That's a lenient judge. Is he on probation?"

"He's out. That's all I care about."

"Does he live at your house?"

"He and my parents don't get along. They don't even know he's out."

"Where does he live?"

"He thinks it's better if I don't know. He comes to see me when my parents aren't around."

"I'd like to meet him."

"You would?"

"Sure. I've never met a real convict." She puts her hands up. "I'm kidding."

"You know," I say, "you kind of remind me of him."

"I do?"

"He's . . . wild, like you. Says what he's thinking, doesn't hold back."

"Now I really want to meet him."

"Well, maybe—"

"Kiss me."

I look at her. "What?"

"Shut up and kiss me." She leans forward and

clamps her mouth on mine. After she pulls back, I try to kiss her again.

She stops me. "Don't you want to know if I'm a dyke?"

"I assumed you weren't."

"Maybe I'm bisexual."

"Are you?"

"Does it matter?"

"No, it doesn't." This time she doesn't stop me as my lips find hers. Softer than anything I've felt before.

"I'm no beauty," she whispers. "I have no fantasies about that. The way I am, the way I dress, that's not going to change. But I like you, Chase, and one thing I won't do is play games. I promise."

"Okay."

"So we'll hang out together?"

"Sure."

"I'm not looking for sex, okay?"

"Yeah."

"I don't care whether or not you're a virgin."

"I am. A virgin," I say.

"You didn't have to tell me."

"I know."

"Just so we know where things stand."

We kiss one more time. "You don't want to be late for therapy," Darla says.

We stand and start walking, holding hands. When we reach the street Dr. Braun's office is on, Darla says good-bye, and I realize after she's left that I have no idea where she lives, whether she has a short or a long walk home.

"Sounds like you told Darla a lot about yourself," Dr. Braun says.

Yes, I did, I'm thinking as I leave her office. And I feel pretty good about it.

Things are beginning to look up.

CHAPTER 10

"I don't think I can do this," Darla says.

"What?"

"This scene, what do you think?"

We're both irritable. Darla because, even though Mr. Hannah gave us extra time to prepare our scene, two weeks have gone by and she still doesn't know her lines.

"Darla, we go on Friday," I remind her.

"I'm sorry."

"All right," I say, sighing, "let's forget it for today."

"You mean it?"

"What the hell, we've got plenty of time. Three whole days."

My sarcasm goes right over her head. The trouble

we're having with the scene is only part of the reason *I* feel irritable.

"I'll memorize my lines tonight," she promises.

"Sure." I give her a hug of reassurance I only half believe.

"Where'd I put my bag?" She starts looking along the row of seats.

We don't have a heavy physical relationship. An occasional kiss and hug, holding hands, that's about it, though everybody in school seems to think there's more to it. Lately I've been wishing there *was*.

Ben hasn't been by. I guess he left town. It hurts, but what can I do?

Mom and Dad haven't talked any more about my skipping auditions. They're back to treating me like the kid in the glass cage. They ask me how I am a lot and go out of their way to talk in calm voices when I'm around.

My therapy plods along. No new shards of memory. Maybe there won't be any more. Last time I was there, Thursday, Dr. Braun looked like she was irritated that she couldn't find more wrong with me.

"I don't think I need to come here anymore," I say.

"Really." Smoking and tapping.

"I feel good. I haven't been counting that much."

"Hell, I guess you're cured."

I look at her, and she stares back. The old trick. I smile.

"Cut that out," she says, breaking the silence for once.

"What?"

"That smug look. It pisses me off."

"What do you mean, 'smug'?"

"Look it up in the dictionary."

"I know what 'smug'—"

"Have you had any new memories lately?"

"No."

"Not since the one about Angie in the car?"

"Come here, Chase, I've got something to show you."

"No."

"Ben still hasn't come by?"

"No."

"Why do you think that is?"

"He's left town."

"Must make you angry."

"He's gotta do what he's gotta do."

"I thought he was supposed to be watching out for you."

"He doesn't have to do anything."

"You don't need him anymore?"

"He stopped by a few times, then moved on. I'm glad I got to see him."

"Think he's got a job somewhere?"

"I don't know."

"Hmm." She finishes her cigarette. "I'd like to talk to you about that dream again."

"Why do we have to—"

"Humor me. Like we said before, there's a lot of good stuff in that dream. A lot of the images—"

"*You* said."

"Pardon me?"

"*You* said there was a lot of good stuff. Not me."

She stares, and says, "This smart-ass side of you is new. What's bringing it on?"

I shrug.

She fishes out another cigarette. "Anyway, a lot of the images make sense. You can connect them with events in your life. Ben jumping off the roof, that's a memory from childhood representing your guilt about the car accident. What I haven't been able to figure out is why you feel guilty toward Ben, or why, in your sub-conscious, your feelings about the car accident connect with that particular incident. If we knew what about the accident you're blocking, we might have the answer."

"Sounds like psychobabble to me."

Ignoring my comment, she continues, "I suspect the people rocking in the sanctuary represent your lack of control, especially where it concerns your family, which is controlled by your dad's profession. The screech of the brakes turning into Angie's scream, that's obvious.

Another example of your guilt over Angie's death."

"You've got it all figured out, why don't you write a paper about it?"

"Actually, there's one thing in the dream I haven't been able to make a connection with."

"Well, I don't want to hear it."

"You don't."

"No. And you know what else? You smoke too much."

"My smoking bothers you?" she says after exhaling.

"Yeah. Well, no, not really. It's just you do it a lot. It's bad for you."

"You're concerned for my health?"

"Maybe."

"It is bad for me. But I can't seem to stop. That's why they call it an addiction."

"Why do you do it?"

"I've done it since I was fourteen," she says. "It's not something I'm particularly proud of."

"But why do you do it? Just 'cause you've done it since you were a kid? What's the psychological reason?"

She puts down the cigarette. "What are you so pissed off about today?"

"You're always analyzing me. What about you?"

"I'm the psychiatrist. You're the patient. That's what I'm being paid for. That's why you came to me."

"I came to you because Dr. McShane told me to."

"Oh, that again."

"Maybe I just don't need you anymore."

Silence. I match her gaze. "All right," she says, taking her notebook from the side table and tossing it onto her cluttered desk. "We haven't accomplished much in the last couple of weeks anyway. Maybe we both need a break." She does the same with her pack of cigarettes. "You've got your wish. No more session today. And you don't have to come Monday, either."

"Just Monday?"

"Sorry, that's all I can promise. You may think you're cured, but I don't. And I'm the one who makes that decision." She stands up. "I'll even move next Thursday's appointment to Friday. That'll give you more than a week till you have to come back. Who knows, maybe the time away will stir some things up." She indicates the door. "See you a week from tomorrow. Same time."

"That's it?" I ask, waiting to find out what the catch is.

"That's it."

Now it's four days later and, for the first time since I started therapy with Dr. Braun, I do not have a Monday afternoon appointment. But I haven't felt right since I walked out of that office. And *that* pisses me off.

But I have enjoyed hanging out with Darla. Even if I don't know if we're girlfriend-boyfriend. It didn't bother me as much until Heather approached me in the hallway after first period.

"How're you doing?" she asks.

I shrug. "Okay. How are rehearsals going?" She got the part of Margaret More like she said she would.

"Just a couple of read-throughs so far. Blocking starts next week. Kyle's going to be a good Thomas More." She pauses. "How's your girlfriend?"

"Darla?" I act indifferent. "She's not my girlfriend, really."

"She's not, huh?"

"We're friends. We talk."

"You can talk to her but not to me?"

"I've got to get to class."

"Everybody talks about you."

"Kids have been talking about me since the accident," I point out. "And since I got out of the hospital."

"No, I mean they've been talking about the two of you. Everybody thinks you're an item. A couple of freaks."

"Who cares what they think?" I start to move around her.

"I do." She puts her hand on my chest. "Because you're my friend, and you've been through too much already. You should care too."

"Why?"

"I found out something about Darla Prince."

"I don't want to hear—"

"You'll want to hear this." She moves closer, looking so comical as her eyes dart left and right, I want to laugh. Until I hear her next words. "She used to be a slut. Maybe still is."

I just stare.

"And not just with boys. Roy has this friend from up around Wilkes-Barre who came down to visit him this past weekend. They were catching up, and this guy told him about a party he was at where this girl, who everybody said had just broken up with another girl, took on a bunch of guys in one of the bedrooms. A real loudmouth, according to Roy's friend. The way he described her, Roy started asking questions. Guess what he found out? The girl was Darla."

I stand there, speechless. I should be saying something. Anything.

"I'd be careful if I was you, Chase." The bell rings. "Gotta get to class."

I should have said something.

But why should I believe Heather? She's made it very clear she doesn't like Darla and me together. It would be just like her to try to split us apart.

But how can I be sure?

"Thanks for being so understanding," Darla says, having found her book bag. She leans in to kiss me, but without thinking, I pull back.

"What?" she asks, surprised. "You mad at me about the lines?"

"No, I . . . No. I'm not."

"You sure? You seem—"

"It's nothing. I'm fine." This time I lean in, and we kiss. Once. Then again, only this time I push for more. Like something has taken control of me. At first she's willing, until my hand finds an opening in the flannel shirt.

"Hey!" she shouts, pushing my hand away. "You've got to ask permission first before you try that, buster."

"Okay," I say. "How about it?"

"No. Definitely not."

"Definitely, huh? Why?"

"Because I said so."

"Because you're a virgin?"

She stares. "What the hell's wrong with you?"

Shut up, Chase! "Nothing. I . . . I just don't know what we are. Are we boyfriend and girlfriend?"

"We're friends."

"Just friends?"

"Friends with benefits."

"We can't be more?"

"Maybe. I don't know yet."

"Okay. I'm sorry."

"Are you all right, Chase?"

Just ask her. Heather's probably lying. Just say, Hey, you were right about Heather. Do you know what she told me?

"I'm feeling weird today, I guess."

"We all have weird days." She touches my arm. "Let's give it some time, okay?"

"Sure." Let it go. Move on.

But I can't. Because what Heather told me is rattling around in my head, like when someone tells you not to think about pink elephants, and it's all you *can* think about.

One-two-three-four. Two-four-six-eight. Breathe. *Three-six-nine-twelve. Four—*

Oh, shit, I can't help myself.

"You know, if you want to stay a virgin, it doesn't mean we can't . . . you know . . ."

"Make out?" Darla finishes.

"Of course," I blurt out, "you never told me you were a virgin." *Stupid, stupid! Why did I just say that?*

Her eyes narrow. "Why is it suddenly so important to you?"

I say nothing. Neither does she. The silence is worse than if she'd just slapped me.

"What have you heard?" she says between clenched teeth.

"Nothing. Why do you—"

"Bullshit." She waits, staring.

"Let's just forget it, okay?" She keeps staring. "It's stupid, I don't know why . . ." *SHUT UP! MAKE UP SOMETHING!* "I heard about this party—"

"Who told you!" she spits in my face. "Wait a minute. I can guess."

She turns and moves quickly out of the auditorium. "Darla? Where are you going?" But I already know. There's no practice today, and Heather always leaves through the main doors. I try to catch up, but Darla's moving so damn fast. Through the main hall and out the front entrance where kids are waiting for buses or their rides, or are hanging out before heading home. And at the far end of the sidewalk, about to turn onto a side street, are Heather and Kyle.

Darla starts running. No one in the crowd is paying attention, so no one sees her spin Heather around and punch her, knocking Kyle to the side in the process, the force of Darla's swing sending her tumbling down on top of Heather. Darla gets in a few more licks before I pull her back. Heather jumps to her feet, blood dribbling from a cut in the corner of her mouth.

"You bitch!" Heather screams.

Darla yanks herself easily from my grasp but doesn't move and, despite her fury, answers Heather in a low controlled voice. "If you're gonna spread rumors about me, you better be ready to answer for them."

"Did you hear that, Kyle? She threatened me. You heard her, Chase."

"You bet I'm threatening you." Darla takes a menacing step, and Heather pushes back against Kyle, who doesn't seem to know what to do. I grab Darla by the arm, but she has already stopped moving. "I hear that you're talking garbage about me one more time, I'll come after you again."

"Keep that freak away from me. You hear me? Put her back in her cage. Freak! Dyke!"

Darla's rage seems to vanish, leaving her as deflated as a balloon. Pointing at Heather, she says, "Remember what I said." Then, with shoulders slumped, she turns and starts walking away.

"You keep that cow on a leash, Chase!" Heather shouts, as kids come running, and I know everyone's going to find out. Turning to Kyle, Heather cries, "How bad is it? How do I look?"

Keeping my distance, I follow Darla. After a while, when it seems like she's never going to acknowledge me, I call out, "Hey." She stops, and I slow down. "Darla?"

"What!" She keeps her back to me.

"Can't we talk about it?"

"You want the dirty details?"

"No," I say. "But what happened? You can tell me."

"I can, huh? What do you want to know? How many guys I did that night? Were there other times?" She turns and faces me. "Yes, there were. Times I'm sorry for. Times I wish I could take back, but I can't."

"I'm sorry, Darla."

"Is that why you tried to feel me up? To see if the rumor was true?"

"No—"

"I told you I wasn't looking for that."

"I know. I'm sorry."

"If you had asked me, I would have told you."

I don't know what to do, how to fix it.

"It was fun while it lasted," she says.

"What does that mean?"

"You know."

"Darla . . . I'm sorry. I made a mistake."

"I'm sorry, Angie. I made a mistake."

"Yes . . ."

"Yes."

". . . you did."

"You did."

"What can I do? Please tell me."

". . . tell me."

"Nothing, Chase."

"There must be something."

She turns and walks off down the street. When she's almost out of sight, I go to call out again, but almost shout Angie's name. I stand there a long time before heading home.

That night the dream Dr. Braun loves returns.

CHAPTER 11

I'm in church, Dad's preaching, and the whole congregation is into it, rocking and swaying. Next to me on the pew my mother has her eyes closed, and she's talking to herself in a low voice as she clutches a Bible to her breasts and sways with the rest of them.

"Look at me, Chase! I'm Superboy!"

As my dad continues to rail from the pulpit, he beckons me forward. But I run the other way and find myself outside of the house we lived in when Uncle Julius was sick and lived next door until he died.

I look up to the roof, and there's Ben wearing a blanket like a cape and standing near the edge, from where he shouts, "Look at me, Chase! I'm Superboy!"

"What are you doing up there?"

"I'm gonna fly!"

"Ben, oh my God, come down from there."

"Son, you climb back into the window right now. Right now! Do you hear me?"

"But I can do it, Dad. I really can!"

"Ben, please . . ."

"I can't be hurt! I'm the boy of steel!"

"Ben, I'm your father, and I'm ordering you . . ."

He spreads the blanket like great wings on a bird . . .

". . . to climb back in that window . . ."

. . . like the arms of Jesus on the crucifix . . .

". . . right this minute!"

. . . leans forward . . .

. . . bends his knees . . .

"Noooo!" my mother screams, her cry stretching out into forever, until it sounds like the screeching of brakes. And then sounds like something else.

Angie.

Screaming.

All at once a stage curtain drops in front of me. Bringing darkness.

I wait. Not sure what to do. Do I stay or do I go?

Someone lines up on my left. Then two more on my right.

I say nothing. We wait.

It's never going to open.

And then it does.

As light fills the stage, I recognize Ben to my left. His arm in a sling, though he is the age he is now, not eleven.

On my right are Angie and Darla.

The stage becomes the backyard where Ben landed from the roof. A path in front of us leads to the house next door.

Darla and Angie look at me, wave sadly, and they walk down off the stage. "Don't," I plead.

Ben starts to follow them.

"Ben . . ."

"Sorry, kiddo, I have to." He turns and, with his good hand, places something in mine.

I look down.

Seeing the broken family crucifix, I scream . . .

And wake up sweating. Mouth open. I listen for any sound from my parents downstairs. Did they hear me yell? Or was it only in my dream?

I close my eyes.

One-two-three-four. Two-four-six-eight. Breathe.

"Hey, kiddo."

"Ben!" After all this time. "Ben."

"Hi, Chase."

I sit up. "Where have you been?"

"I wasn't far," he says.

"How'd you get in?"

"Same way as before."

"Chase! It's seven thirty!" Mom with the first warning.

"I need your help, LB."

He's different. Gone is the cavalier attitude. The easy smile. His grin is more a grimace. He looks as if he hasn't slept. The skin below his eyes is pale and sunken.

"Help with what?" I ask.

"I got in with some guys I shouldn't have, and now I'm in trouble." He lets out a deep sigh. "I had it worked out. One easy score and I'd have enough money to get away from here. A fresh start."

"What happened?"

"You don't want to know. Just . . . help me."

"How?"

"I need money."

"I only have fifty bucks, maybe."

"That's not enough."

"It's all I've got."

"Mom and Dad have some."

I stare at him.

"Doesn't Mom still have her 'rainy day' money? For emergencies? I just don't know where she keeps it here . . . I need that money, Chase."

"I don't know . . ."

"I can't stay away from those guys for long."

"What do they want?" I ask.

"Just tell me where she keeps it. Or you could get it for me."

Mom calls again. "Chase? Are you awake? It's time to get up."

"I'm up!" I shout back. "I'll be down in a minute!"

To my brother: "I'll do my best—"

"Thanks—"

"But there's something else I want to talk about."

Ben frowns. "What?"

I swallow hard. "I want to tell."

"Look, after I've left, you can tell them. I'll be gone."

"I'm not talking about that."

Ben says nothing. I hear movement downstairs, and for a terrible moment it sounds like Mom or Dad is breaking tradition and coming up to check on me. But the noise stops.

"We talked about this."

"We should have told them a long time ago," I say. "Things might have been different."

"Mom and Dad don't want you to tell them," Ben says. "Better their little world is not disrupted. Say a prayer and all the problems go away. Hang a crucifix and the truth stays hidden forever."

"But they might have done something."

"I doubt it." He looks at me. "But it's not your fault."

"Yes, it is. I knew why you always got into trouble."

"Don't try to get in my head, little brother."

"I know why you beat up that old guy."

"Stop it."

"If I'd just told them—"

"Nothing would have happened, damn it! Not then, not now! Don't you get it? They're scared of us. Me 'cause I've always been bad. Bad enough to get sent to prison. But they're more scared of you, Chase, 'cause you're so pissed at them, you tried to kill yourself."

He grabs me by the shoulders. "Shit. I don't like getting angry at you. I love you." He takes a deep breath. "Going to them now won't do any good. If there's anyone to blame, it's me."

"I don't want you to go, Ben."

"Breakfast is on the table, Chase!" Dad's turn.

"I don't want to go either, Chase. But I have to. I paid my debt. But I screwed up again. So I've got to go." He gives me a fierce hug. "Now get your shoes on before Mom and Dad start wondering why you're not down there. I'll sneak out like I did before."

"Ben—"

"Come on."

"I'll get the money."

"I've changed my mind. Forget it."

"I'll do it."

"No."

"Those men will kill you, won't they?"

He looks at me.

"Let me help you!"

After a moment Ben asks, "Are you sure?"

"Yes."

"I'll make it up to you."

"No. Once you get away from here, you should never come back. Where can I meet you with the money?"

"How about the playground at the elementary school on Spencer? Tonight. Can you get out?"

"I'll make up something."

He smiles. "I owe you, Chase."

"No, Ben. I owe you. I always have."

I sit on the bed and pull on my sneakers.

In the kitchen I hear the front door click shut.

Dad's going to his office, but Mom's actually going to be home until noon. Then she has a lunch meeting. Dad has an afternoon hospital visit, and Mom is getting together with a friend after lunch. They'll both be home around dinnertime. I'll get the money before then.

Tonight I'll make up an excuse to go out. I'll give my brother the money. I'll tell him good-bye.

Forever.

CHAPTER 12

All I can think about at school is where Mom keeps her "rainy day" money. In a can hidden behind a set of dishes we don't use.

I picture what might happen to Ben if I don't get the money. On the ground, bloody, surrounded by faceless men.

I have to help him. I *have* to.

The school day takes forever. I see Darla heading for fourth period at the other end of the hall. I try to catch up, but I get pushed into the lockers. My books tumble to the floor.

Mitch and Lars face me, grinning. "Gee, I'm sorry, I didn't see you," Lars says. "Let me get those." He picks up my books and makes as if to give them to me. But when I reach for them, he drops them.

"Can you be any more freaking clumsy, Lars?" Mitch laughs. I go to pick them up.

"Hey, don't let him squat in front of you like that," Mitch shouts. "You don't know what he might do down there."

I straighten back up with the books. They move closer. Now I can't move without bumping into them.

"Where's your girlfriend?" Lars asks.

"Found herself a girl she likes better, maybe." Mitch grins.

A small group has formed to watch us. "Please let me pass," I ask, hating the way my voice is trembling.

"What do you mean, 'pass'?" Mitch says. "Like pass gas? You gotta go to the bathroom?" Lars laughs like it's the funniest thing he's ever heard.

"I've got class." Trying to sidestep them, I bump Lars's shoulder.

"Hey! I felt that."

"I think you should apologize," Mitch says.

"I . . . I'm sorry."

"I didn't hear you." Mitch holds his hand to his ear. "Say it again."

"I'm sorry."

"I don't know if that's good enough. Is that good enough, Lars?"

"No," Lars says. "I don't think he meant it."

"Try again. Mean it this time."

Again, I try to move. Mitch pushes me back. "We're not finished—"

"What's going on here?" Mr. Hannah appears through the crowd of kids, who scatter quickly.

"Nothing," Mitch says. "We're just talking."

"I wonder if your wrestling coach would think you were just talking. Or better yet, the principal, if I told him what I just witnessed and recommended you sit out the first few wrestling meets."

"We're going, Mr. Hannah," Lars says. "Come on, Mitch."

The two hurry off. The hall's now empty.

"Are you all right?" Mr. Hannah asks.

"Yeah," I answer. "It was no big deal."

"I don't know about that. I *should* say something to the principal—"

"Don't. It's not necessary."

"Well . . . if they bother you again . . . My theatre kids get enough flack."

"Thanks for helping me out." I start to go.

"Actually, I need to tell you something. Darla Prince dropped drama class."

I look at him. "You won't be able to do your scene. I was thinking I could give you extra time. You could practice a Thomas More scene with Rachel, since she's playing More's wife."

She didn't have to drop out. We could've—

"What do you think?"

"I, uh, think that'd be too weird," I answer. "I don't want Kyle to think . . ."

"Yeah, you're right." He puts his hand on my shoulder. "I'm sorry, Chase."

"I'll be all right."

"See you in class."

The day continues to drag. I see my new wrestling team buddies. The first time, they give me limp-wristed waves. The second time, one of them shouts, "I heard your girlfriend quit drama class for weight lifting."

From the other: "Does she have hair on her tits, Shakespeare?"

Not seeing Darla in class makes me feel empty. Heather's not there either, and she's supposed to do her scene today. I keep to myself while the other scheduled scene goes on. Following the critique, Mr. Hannah tells us to do homework.

The minute hand creeps around the auditorium clock.

The moment the bell rings, I'm up and out of the school as fast as possible. Normally it would take me thirty minutes to walk the two miles home, but if I hurry, I can do it in close to twenty. A block from school, I start to jog. Mom and Dad shouldn't be home before dinner, but what if something unexpected happens and they get home sooner? I wonder how Ben plans to travel? He wouldn't be flying. Too expensive. He'll probably take a bus or train. Maybe he'll rent a car. Hopefully, there'll be enough money to get him far away from here.

I settle into a rhythm, my feet pounding the sidewalk. Missing the cracks. I turn onto another street. Pass houses that all look the same. Reminding me of the neighborhood where the police found me the night of the accident. Why did I drink so much that night? I hardly drink at all.

Maybe I was just missing Angie. Getting drunk gave me an excuse to call her. I took advantage of her goodwill. Which means, because of me—

The headlights bear down on us, and Angie turns, an awful certainty showing in her face. She knows she's about to die and there's nothing she can do.

She reaches for me . . .

Something hits me from behind, and I fall to my knees. As I gasp for air, hands lift me to my feet. "Aw, gee, I'm sorry," a familiar voice says.

"You keep bumping into this guy." The other voice familiar too. "Must be karma or something."

"What're you running for?" Lars. Or maybe Mitch. They're interchangeable.

"Maybe he's trying out for the track team."

"I don't think they take faggots on the track team."

"You're right. I think they only take faggots in drama class."

"Homo class, you mean."

"Look . . ." I stop; breathe.

Lars steps in front of me. "You say something?"

"Where's your girlfriend?" Mitch to my right.

Slowly, I straighten up.

"Maybe he's running 'cause he can't wait to see her."

"Do you think she's got a pussy and a dick under those dyke clothes?"

"Look," I try again. Breathing easier. "I've got to get home."

"Why?" Mitch asks.

"Maybe his boyfriend's waiting for him."

"You mean Darla? Or a guy? Or is she a guy? I get confused."

I notice a few kids gathered at the corner across the street, some laughing and pointing. Waiting to see what happens next.

I try to walk away, but, predictably, the two block my path.

"So go," Mitch says, grinning that stupid grin. "We ain't stopping you."

I try again. Again, they stop me. "What are you waiting for?"

"You're not letting me."

"He's screwing with us," Lars says.

"Watch saying 'screw' around this guy. You don't know what he might do."

"I need to get home."

"Home to Mommy? She gonna kiss your boo-boo for you?" Mitch makes loud kissing noises.

"Please—"

"Aw. He said, 'please.'"

"Say it again." Lars pushes me.

"Will you let me go?"

"Maybe."

Anything to get out of here. "Please."

"Please what?"

"Please let me go," I say, sounding pitiful.

"I don't think he means it, Mitch."

"I think you're right."

"What do you want me to do?" I ask. Ashamed. But I need to get the money for Ben.

Mitch turns to Lars. "What do you think?"

"Strip."

I look at him. "What . . . ?"

"Take off your clothes. We'll let you go if you walk home naked."

I glance back at the small crowd.

Lars smiles. "I've always been curious if homos are built the same as normal guys."

If Ben were here, he'd know what to do. "You want to see what I look like . . . naked?"

"I'm sure those kids are curious too. Especially the girls."

He definitely wouldn't put up with this crap.

"Come on, Lars, he's not gonna care about girls."

"There are a couple of pretty good-looking guys, too."

He'd do something about it.

"Yeah," I say, my voice sounding different. More like Ben's voice. Because he's the kind that stands up to stupid bullies. "But none of them are as good-looking as you."

Mitch's grin drops. "What'd you say?"

First, Ben would play with them.

"I didn't know you guys were one of us," I tease, unbuttoning my shirt. "I've heard rumors about wrestlers . . . They like to wear tights and get real close and personal when they wrestle."

Lars has stopped smiling too. His eyes are narrow slits.

"I'm not going to have time to do both of you, though." I drop my shirt to the ground.

"Do?" From Mitch.

"How about you, Lars? You look ready."

And he'd watch, wait. Ready to move in for the kill.

"Mitch, you'll have to wait until tomorrow." I work my belt. "How about after school in the light booth of the auditorium? Not a lot of room there, but it's real cozy—"

When Lars swings first, I'm ready for him. Ducking his fist, I grab his arm and twist as hard as I can. The wrestler gives a high-pitched scream, loses his balance, and falls. Mitch swings next, and my chest explodes. He swings again, missing me, but we both go down in a tangle. I get to my knees first, and as Mitch tries to get up, I push him face-first into the sidewalk. Then Lars blind-sides me, and the two of us go rolling. Somehow I end up on top and begin wailing on him, his hands up to protect himself. I bat them away and keep hitting him.

Suddenly a tank hits me. Mitch growling like a bear, spitting blood and shouting, "You son of a bitch!" He starts slapping me, his hands a blur.

"Get him up," I hear Lars say, and Mitch pulls me to my feet, almost yanking my arm out of the socket. Mitch pins my arms from behind while Lars grabs me by the throat. "First I'm gonna rip your throat out," he hisses. "Then I'm gonna skin you alive." He begins to squeeze. I can't breathe. I begin to see lights dance in my peripheral vision. Growing larger.

"Enough!" All at once, the pressure is gone. Mitch lets me go. I fall to my knees, retching.

"What the hell do you think you're doing?"

"He was coming on to us. We had to do something!"

"Yeah, right, Lars. I'm sure he was hot for you."

"No, really—"

"We were teaching him a lesson—"

"From the look of your face, Mitch, it looks like he taught you the lesson."

Gentle hands this time take hold of me. "Can you stand, Farrell?"

Kevin Harris.

I open my eyes.

"Are you all right?" he asks.

"Yeah," I manage.

"We were standing up for you," Lars explains.

"And he did come on to us," Mitch adds. "We were just fooling with him, and he said he wanted to do me in the light booth. Ask those kids over there. I'm sure they heard."

Kevin looks back over his shoulder at the thinning crowd. "You were standing up for me?"

"'Cause he wouldn't tell you about the accident."

He turns. "Are you sure you're okay, Farrell?"

I nod and pick up my shirt.

"See?" Mitch complains. "He took his shirt off. That proves he was coming on—"

"Shut up! You ever try this again, you'll answer to me. Now get out of here."

"You're not thinking straight, Kevin," Mitch says.

"I'm thinking fine."

Mitch turns to me. "If you think this is the end of it—"

Kevin goes right in Mitch's face. "That's exactly what it is. The end. Now leave before *I* beat the crap out of you."

Mitch backs down quickly, and he and Lars head off in the direction of the school.

The two of us stand uncomfortably, saying nothing. I finish buttoning my shirt.

"Are you sure you're all right?" Kevin says finally.

"Yeah," I tell him.

"I can't believe those guys would . . . You're not gonna have to worry about them again, I promise you."

"I have to get home."

"Sure. Listen, can I walk with you a minute?"

I look at him.

"Just for a minute."

I hesitate, then nod.

A couple of minutes pass without him saying anything.

"Look, Kevin, there's nothing more I can tell you."

"I know."

"Then what—"

"I've been thinking about what you said before . . . the look on Angie's face when she knew she was going to die. . . ."

Kevin looks at me. "I'm sorry, Chase," he says. "I've been an asshole. Worrying about the fact I wasn't there to save her. As if I could have done anything. The thing is, I loved her. But I know you still loved her too. The fact that you were there right next to her when it happened . . . Well, maybe it's better that you don't remember all of it."

I just listen. "She talked about you, you know. A lot. I think she still had a thing for you. It made me jealous."

I feel something give inside me.

"I meant what I said. Those guys won't bother you anymore. I won't bother you either." Kevin extends his hand. "You're a good guy, Chase. I know that because of Angie."

Slowly, I take his hand.

"Good luck." He looks back only once to wave as he walks away.

Mom and Dad aren't home, and I get the money, no problem. Five hundred dollars. I have an ugly bruise on my neck courtesy of Lars. Digging through my clothes, I pull out a turtleneck Mom bought me that I never wear.

At dinner it's hard to eat. I move the food around on my plate.

"Aren't you hungry, Chase?"

"Sure, Dad." I take a ridiculously large bite of mashed potatoes and peas, smiling while I chew.

"What made you put on that shirt?" Mom asks. "I thought you didn't like it."

"I just decided to wear it." Another huge bite. Maybe they won't expect me to talk if my mouth is full.

"It hasn't been turtleneck weather," Dad says. "I wonder when fall's really going to get here."

"Won't be long before winter," Mom says. "I could buy you some more."

"Sure," I respond, grinning and chewing. The money is in my jeans pocket because I couldn't think of any other safe place to put it. I keep feeling for the wad of bills, checking to make sure they haven't slipped out somehow. I keep expecting Dad to blurt out something like *We sure could use that rainy day money, Beth. Why don't you go check to see how much is in there?*

After dinner I head up to my room to do nothing for half an hour. I don't want to look too anxious. I'm on edge, expecting to hear Mom scream, *The emergency money's gone!*

But nothing happens, and I come out of my room and sneak silently down into the kitchen.

I hear my parents talking in the family room. "I think he's better, Mary Beth. Don't you?"

"He's nervous all the time."

"I had a lot of energy when I was a teenager."

"I'm not talking about just energy, Matt. I think his therapy's the problem. It's not helping."

"I think it is."

"You always say things are better, because you want them to be."

"That's not fair."

I should go. "Mom? Dad? I'm going for a walk. Be back soon."

Silence. I head toward the front door.

"We're almost finished with our card game," Dad calls back. "Wait ten minutes, and we'll come with you."

Shit. I hadn't thought of that possibility. "I'd rather go by myself if it's okay with you. Be back soon."

Silence. Then: "Don't take too long."

"Okay." The wad of cash feels like a hot coal in my pocket.

I pass the mantel in the living room. Stop to check. Turn to go.

But I can't. I check again.

Nothing broken. Good. *One-two-three-four. Two-four-*

six-eight. Breathe. Up to sixteen. Breathe again.

It's never been this bad. I have to get it just right. If I miss anything, something terrible will happen.

Check. The crucifix looks fine. *One-two-three-four. Two-four-six-eight.* Breathe. *Three-six-nine-twelve. Four-eight-twelve-sixteen.* Better. Now get going. Ben is waiting—

"Do it!"

Coming from behind me. My hand on the door-knob, I hear it again.

"Do it!"

It's coming from the figure on the cross. Dr. McShane told me if I ever heard the voice again to call Dr. Braun immediately. But I have to get to Ben.

"Come here, Chase, I've got something to show you."

I freeze.

"Aren't you gonna check again?"

I look. It hasn't moved. Hasn't changed.

I count. Move.

Reach for the doorknob.

"That girl's right."

"What . . . girl?"

"Darla. Your latest romantic failure. Really blew that one, didn't you?"

This isn't real.

"You might as well have called her a whore. Of course, you could apologize. But you and I both know you're not very good

with the people you care about. Ask Angie. And Ben. Five hundred bucks isn't gonna help him. Your brother's doomed."

"Shut up!"

"All his troubles could have been avoided if only you'd told somebody. Mr. Keeper of Secrets."

I see myself at the age of nine standing at a door. Scared to death. Because I know what's on the other side.

And the figure of Jesus hangs above me.

"Do it!"

Now I'm in Angie's car, headlights bearing down, bathing us in a light so bright, I can see the awful acceptance on Angie's face. She knows she's going to die.

"I said, do it!"

She reaches for me . . .

"You did it before, you can do it again."

Now I'm in front of that door again.

"Get it over with!"

Listening to what's on the other side.

"Cut your lousy wrists!"

I feel the weight in my pocket. Reach in and pull out . . .

Not the money. A razor blade.

"Do it right this time."

"Shut up! Leave me alone!"

"Do it."

"No."

"Do it!"

"I said leave me alone! Leave—"

"Chase? What's going on?"

My parents are here. Staring at me like I'm a dangerous animal that has just escaped from his cage.

"Chase?" Mom says again.

I don't move.

"Whom were you yelling at?" Dad asks in a hushed voice.

"I wasn't . . . No one." He doesn't ask if I'm okay.

"We heard you talking. Yelling."

"I . . . I've gotta go out."

"Where?"

"A walk—"

"Chase," Mom cuts in. "What's that in your hand?"

I look down. What I thought was a razor blade is now the wad of money.

"Where did you get—?" Mom falters. "Is that the 'rainy day' money?"

There's nothing for me to say. If I'd just gotten out of here a couple of minutes earlier.

"The emergency money?"

"I can't . . ."

"Why?"

"It's for Ben!"

Stunned, Mom and Dad stare at me. Saying nothing.

"He's been out for a while. He's been coming to see me. I was taking this money to him. He needs it."

"Ben comes to see you?" Dad says. "You've been talking to him?"

"Yes, damn it! I'm sorry; I didn't mean to curse. It's just . . . he's in trouble. That's all I can tell you. He needs to get out of town. But if he came back, you'd take him in, wouldn't you? You'd forgive him? He's done his time. He—"

"Stop it!" Mom cries out. "Is this some kind of joke?"

I look at her.

"Mary Beth," Dad says, "I'm sure there's an explanation—"

"No! There can't be an 'explanation.' Not for this." Holding back tears. "I can't deal with this, Matt. I can't—" She turns suddenly and hurries out of the room.

"Give me the money," Dad says, putting out his hand.

"If I don't get this to Ben—"

"That's enough about Ben! Give it to me!"

"Or you'll what? You never gave him a chance! You're a minister. You're supposed to forgive—"

"How dare you!" I think he's going to hit me.

Instead, he takes a deep breath. "Please. Give it to me, Chase."

"But—"

"Please."

"Dad—"

"Go to your room. Go to your room now!"

His look scares me. "Dad . . ."

I slap the bills into his hand, open the front door, and run outside. I don't know what I can do without the money, but maybe together Ben and I can figure out some place for him to hide until we find him some cash.

I still see that door. Jesus above me.

I run faster.

CHAPTER 13

"I'm gonna smoke, do you mind? I know—it's a filthy habit."

This is the last place I expected to be this morning. The last thing I expected my parents to do.

Call Dr. Braun.

Ben wasn't at the playground. I waited a long time, but he never showed. More likely, he'd waited as long as he could before I got there.

When I got back, Mom and Dad said they'd called Dr. Braun and made an appointment. And they were going to make sure I got there even if they had to carry me to her office. They even called the school and said I wouldn't be in today.

Dr. Braun busies herself opening the window behind her and lighting up.

What if I said I did mind? Would she really not smoke?

I don't ask. The way I feel, I wouldn't care if she put the cigarette out on my face. I've let my brother down. After all he's done for me. What if those men have found him? What if he's lying beaten and bloody somewhere?

"Sounds like things were real interesting in your house last night."

"I don't know why they called you," I mutter. "Mom thinks the therapy isn't helping."

"They're concerned."

I give her a smirk; look away.

"Does that surprise you?"

I just shrug.

"Sounds like you scared the hell out of them."

"What'd they tell you?"

"That you were talking to yourself."

I raise my hand. "Guilty as charged."

"And that you tried to steal five hundred dollars."

"Too bad it wasn't a rainy day."

"What did you need it for?"

"They didn't tell you?"

"I want you to."

I hesitate. "I was planning to give it to Ben."

"Why?"

"He needs it."

"For what?"

"He's in trouble, okay? Some guys he pulled a job with . . . they're after him. I was going to take it to him so he could get away. He didn't show."

"How did your parents react when you told them?"

"They freaked. Bringing up his name in their presence was a big betrayal on my part. When all I want . . ." I falter; take a breath. "All I want is for them to forgive him."

"That's important to you, isn't it?"

"Yes," I say quietly.

"Why do you think Ben didn't show up?"

"He probably did but couldn't wait long. If I'd gotten out before my parents . . . I'm sure he's gone now. He probably . . ."

"What?" A whisper.

"He probably doesn't trust me anymore."

"And that's also important to you."

"Yeah. But, again, I didn't come through for him."

"What you were trying to do was difficult."

"I hope he got away. I hope he's not . . ."

"What?" Dr. Braun asks. "Dead?"

I nod my head.

"What will you do if he is?"

"He has to be okay," I say.

"Or?"

"What do you mean?"

"Would you be able to handle it?"

"I'd be upset. I'd be . . . very, very upset."

"And sad?"

"Of course."

"And alone."

I look at her. "Yes."

"But you'd be alive," she says. "And after a long time of grieving, you'd be ready to move forward. That's what happens when people we love die, Chase. We grieve, sometimes for a couple of years. Then we move on. And you will with Angie and Dan and the others who died in that car crash. As you will with your brother."

It takes a moment for what she said to sink in. "What do you mean, my brother? Did you hear something?"

Slowly, she rises and picks up something from the desk.

"Is that today's newspaper?" I ask. Sweating. "I thought about that. If something had happened to Ben, it'd be in the newspaper. But I looked, and there was nothing. I looked at every page."

"This is a newspaper, Chase," Dr. Braun says. "But not today's." She pulls up a different chair and sits next to me.

Having her so close makes me more nervous.

One-two-three-four.

"Your parents gave this to me this morning."

Two-four-six-eight. Breathe.

"It's from this past January. From the last town you lived in. There's a story here about a fight between residents at a youth detention center."

Threesixninetwelve. Foureighttwelvesixteen. Breathe.

"It says, even though the guards got it under control quickly . . ."

No. Start over!

". . . two inmates were killed."

"I don't want to read that—"

"Chase . . ."

"Please, don't make me read that—"

"One of them was your brother."

"No," I cry. Not able to stop her words.

"Ben Farrell."

"No!"

"Nobody here knew he died, did they," she says. "Nobody even knew you had a brother, much less one in prison. Because you weren't allowed to talk about him. Your parents didn't want anyone to know you had a family member in jail."

"Stop it!"

"Why?"

"I can't talk about it . . ."

"Why? It makes you mad?"

"No . . ."

"Why not? You have every right."

"But . . ." I stand up. "It doesn't do any good."

"Has it been better to hold it in all this time? Pretend it's not there?"

"Maybe."

"No. Never."

"Just shut up."

"Sorry," she says. "Not this time. Let me have it."

"Let you . . . ?"

"Tell me who you're mad at."

"You!"

"Just me?"

I stand there, unable to move. Hands clenched at my sides.

"Come on, who else?"

I can't help myself. "Mom and . . ."

"Mom and Dad?"

"No, I . . . They don't deserve it."

"Why? Because Ben died? Does that give them the right to keep you from talking about him? Not to your friends, not to anyone?"

"They did the best they could."

"I'm not so sure."

"Yes, they did. Ben was . . ."

"What? Hard to live with?"

I say nothing.

"Maybe you're mad at him, too."

All at once the room feels like it's closing in. "No."

"Are you sure?"

"Shut up."

"He was stupid enough to commit a violent crime."

"He wouldn't have if I'd . . ."

"What?"

"I've got to get out of here."

"If you'd what?"

I head for the door.

"Where are you going?"

Stop. Turn around. "I told you to . . ."

"Chase . . . ?"

Moving toward her, I shout, "Shut up! Shut up, *bitch*!" And shove one of the piles off Dr. Braun's desk.

The flying pages feel like my insides exploding, hitting the wall.

I wait. Trembling. Nothing but silence. What is Dr. Braun waiting for?

"Feel better?" I hear her say.

"Your files."

"It's okay. I can clean them up later. More important, I want to know what you're feeling right now."

"I don't—"

"Yes, you do."

After a moment: "It hurts."

"Feelings can be like that. Despite everything we do to try to avoid it."

"I don't want to talk about it anymore," I say, my voice hoarse.

"That's okay. For now," Dr. Braun says in a quiet voice. "But I do want to say one thing. After Ben died, the three of you went back, had a quiet funeral. But when you returned, there was no one to help you grieve. Not your parents, who refused to talk about him. Not your friends. Not even Angie, the girl you loved. Then the accident happened. And then you had her death and the death of the others to deal with. It was too much. You tried to kill yourself. When it didn't work, you came up with the next best thing. You brought your brother back to life. That was very resourceful of you, Chase."

I look at her.

"You found a way to survive. Not everybody can do that. I'm glad you did."

"You are?"

"Sure. I like you very much, Chase."

"I'm sorry I called you a bitch."

"It's okay. I'm fine."

"What now?"

"It's time to start grieving. For real this time."

"I don't know what to do."

"Have you cried for your brother?" she asks. "I mean, really cried?"

If only I could *cry,* I tell myself.

"I don't have another appointment for a couple of hours. If it's any help, I've got plenty of tissues."

If only I could cry, I tell myself, wiping my eyes. My hand comes away wet. Amazed, I look at it. Where have the tears been all this time? Magically, two full boxes of tissues appear on the arm of my chair. Followed by Dr. Braun's arm around my shoulder.

And not even the stale smell of cigarettes can stop me from crying for my lost brother, Ben.

I have no idea how much time has passed. I feel tired, washed out. Dr. Braun has settled back in her chair. The files and loose papers are still on the floor.

"How do you feel?" she asks.

"I don't know," I answer. "Both good and lousy, I guess."

"I believe that."

"My parents told you?"

"Yes. They talked to me before you started your

therapy, of course. Told me then that you had a brother in prison. But not that he'd died there. Though I have to admit, some things weren't adding up. Your brother getting out as soon as he did, considering the severity of the crime, for one thing. It was wrong of your parents not to tell me sooner. They realize that now."

She leans in. There's no cigarette in her hand. In fact, I don't think she's lit one since the first cigarette she smoked after I got here. "There's something else I want to ask you, if you're up to it. Now that we've talked about what happened to your brother, I'm wondering if it's had any effect on your memories concerning the accident. Is there anything more you remember?"

I try to think, try to grab the pieces I've got so far and see what they form. "No," I say. "Well, one thing, but it was before today. I remember Angie reaching for me."

"Really? In the car?"

"Yes."

"Reaching for you how? Like she wanted to hold you? Because she was scared?"

"I don't know."

"Okay. Anything else?"

"No."

"I have another question. Why do you think you cheated on Angie with Heather? You don't seem to me the kind of person who'd do that."

"I don't know."

"I think you do. Deep down inside."

Silence.

"I always felt," I finally say in a quiet voice, "that I didn't deserve . . . what she was giving me, that I didn't deserve *her*."

"You figured something was bound to go wrong?"

I nod.

"Maybe to save yourself from the anxiety of waiting for what you thought was inevitable, you made it happen yourself."

Just like with Darla, I realize.

"I wonder why you think that way about yourself?"

I say nothing.

"In your dream—"

"You like that dream, don't you?" I allow myself a nervous laugh.

"Yeah, I do. There's something in there about everything we've talked about. But I wonder if there's a part of the dream we haven't talked about."

Suddenly I can see the door again.

"You know, Chase, we're dealing with fragments here. Pieces that, by themselves, are hard to understand. But if we could figure out how they fit together . . ."

She pauses, studying me for a moment. "When you were talking about not getting to the playground in time, you said you had let your brother down *again*."

"No, I didn't."

"Yes, you did. You used that word—again."

"I really don't think so."

Another pause, and just when I think she's doing the silent game again, she says, "Let's talk about where you were living when your brother jumped off the roof and broke his arm."

"Why?"

"Why not? You've lived in a number of houses growing up, right?"

"Yeah."

"Anything unusual about this house?"

"No. It was a parsonage, owned by the church that Dad was serving at the time. Like most of the others."

"How tall was the house? Two stories, three? High enough that he could have seriously hurt himself?"

"Well, yeah, I guess. But Ben was always fooling around like that. Doing dangerous stuff."

"Did you actually *see* him fall?"

"He called my name . . ."

"Look at me, Chase. I'm Superboy!"

". . . and I came out."

"Like in your dream."

"Yeah. Mom and Dad came out right after me."

"Did the fall knock Ben unconscious?"

"No. He was in pain. It was clear his arm was broken. We took him to the hospital."

"Did he get special treatment from your parents after that?"

"Sure, he had a broken arm."

"What kind of special treatment?"

I suddenly can't stop fidgeting. "I think Mom and Dad did some special things for him. You know, like parents do when one of their kids is sick."

Another long stare, then she asks, "Is there anything in particular they did for him that pissed you off? That seemed unfair?"

One-two-three-four.

"Chase?"

Two-four-six-eight. "Nothing I can think of."

"Come on, I think there is. I can tell just by the way you're acting."

Breathe. "Yeah, one thing. He didn't have to do his chores."

"His chores," she says, studying me. "Did you have to do them?"

"A lot of them."

"You were how old, nine?"

"Yeah."

"What chores—"

"Come here, Chase—"

"Look, I don't want to talk anymore, okay? You got me to admit my brother's dead, isn't that enough for one day?"

She looks at me, puzzled. I just want to leave. All at once she leans back and says, "You're right. That is a lot to deal with. And we do have your regularly scheduled appointment day after tomorrow. So go home."

I hesitate. "You don't think I need to go back into the hospital?"

"I considered it, and if you want me to admit you, I will. But your parents have told me they'll keep a close eye on you, and to be honest, I want them to. With strict orders that if something happens, they're to call me. So, if you don't want to live at home like that for a while, tell me now. I'll call Dr. McShane."

Thinking about it, I say, "Going back there feels like a step backward now. No, I'm okay with staying at home."

She nods. "If you need me between now and our next appointment, feel free to call me anytime, day or night."

"Okay. Thanks. I appreciate it."

She smiles. Then says, "By the way, when your mom and dad found you talking to yourself, they said you were upset. Since you were on your way to see Ben, you weren't talking to him, I assume. Was it the 'do it' voice, Chase?"

If I tell her yes, maybe she'll change her mind about

the hospital. Or start asking more questions that I don't want to answer.

"No, it wasn't," I tell her, keeping my voice steady. "I was just yelling at myself. All that guilt stuff I can't seem to get rid of, you know?"

I'm not sure she believes me. "Remember, anything comes up, no matter what time it is, call me. See you Friday."

I nod and leave her office.

During the ride home, my parents hardly speak, though my Dad acts like he wants to, and almost does a couple of times. As I watch the road, I think about Ben.

He's gone. Really gone this time. And maybe I'm just cried out, but I don't feel devastated about it anymore.

Maybe, I tell myself, I'm getting better.

CHAPTER 14

It's finally dark outside. I've spent most of the time in my room since coming home. Mom and Dad let me eat my dinner here in private but did stop by a couple of times. To see if I needed anything. So they said.

The telephone rings. Dad calls up to say it's for me.

Dr. Braun. "Just thought I'd see how you're doing."

"All the sharp objects have been put away. My parents let me out of the straitjacket so I could talk to you."

"I'm glad to hear you've developed a sense of humor."

"I have to have something now that you've taken my brother away from me."

"Ouch. Is that what you think?"

After a moment: "Maybe a little bit."

"We can talk about that on Friday."

"Okay." I pause. "Dr. Braun?"

"Yes?"

"You think it's okay for me to go to school?"

"If you feel up to it."

I let out a long sigh.

"It's important to keep moving, Chase," she says. "Even if it's slow. One step at a time."

I nod even though she can't see it.

"And remember, call me if you need to."

"Okay."

"Get a good's night sleep."

What do I do now? Go to sleep early? Watch TV? Read a book? I can't settle on anything.

I lie on my bed. Not thinking about anything in particular. Listening. For the sound of Ben throwing a pebble at my window. For the voice of Jesus to get on my case. Should I tell Dr. Braun about that next time I see her?

God, I miss Ben. What am I going to do without him?

"Chase?" My mother is standing in the doorway. I didn't even hear the door open. "Am I disturbing you?"

"I'm just lying here."

"If you want me to leave . . ."

"What do you want, Mom?"

She looks miserable. "I just wanted to . . . to apologize." Her voice keeps trembling. I'm not sure I've ever seen her like this. "Chase, you must be furious with us. You have every right to be. Your father and I did a terrible thing to you. We realize that now, and we're sorry. I thought if I could explain . . ."

"You don't have to," I tell her.

"Yes, I do. I need to. I owe it to you." She stands very still as she says, "I don't want you to hate us."

That makes me sit up.

"I'd understand if you did. If you want to curse at me, go ahead. That's what Ben would have done. . . ."

I stare, thinking, *That must have been real hard for you, Mom. Saying his name.*

"We spent so much time worrying about him," she says. "We prayed every night Ben would be safe. We never had to worry about you. You always went out of your way to please us. You two couldn't have been more opposite."

She indicates the space on the bed next to me. "May I?"

When I nod, she sits. "After your brother . . . After the funeral, I couldn't stand it. The only way I could deal with it—the *only* way—was to pretend Ben had never existed. People here didn't know about him, so that made it easier. If I could make myself believe he'd never lived, that meant he didn't die. I know that sounds cruel. Crazy. I *was* crazy. With grief."

"You were just trying to survive," I hear myself say. "We both were. You did it by pretending he never lived. I did it by pretending he never died."

We look at each other. Connected in a way I've never felt before.

A long time ago I decided my mother and I had nothing in common. But in fact, we do. We share an almost supernatural ability to survive.

"Why didn't Dad come in here too?" I ask.

"I'm sure he'll talk to you soon. It's very hard for him right now."

Hard, I think. Hard for *him.*

"But there's something we both agree on, Chase. We want you to feel free to talk about Ben anytime you want. *Any* time. All right? Can you forgive us, Chase?"

I put my arm around her. Something I haven't done since before Ben went to jail. Is this forgiveness or just a reflex? I'm not sure I understand what forgiveness is. A strange admission for a preacher's kid. But, for now, holding my mother like this seems right.

CHAPTER 15

"Are you okay?" Dad asks.

"You don't have to keep asking me that."

He looks at me, surprised. "All right." Unsure now, he says, "Do you feel like going to school? You don't have to if you don't want to."

"I want to."

"What should I fix for breakfast?" Mom says. Her voice sounds more high-pitched than usual. "Whatever you want."

Mom makes pancakes.

"How about a ride to school?"

"Sure," I tell her. "Why not?"

"How about you, Matt? Can I give you a ride to the church?"

"If you have time."

At the mantel, I stare at the crucifix. Nothing. No voice. Nothing broken. I do the ritual and head upstairs.

In the car I decide to test Mom's promise. "You know what I've been remembering?" I ask. "That time Ben jumped off the roof and broke his arm. He was eleven. Do you remember?"

Mom and Dad look at each other in the front seat. Dad says, "Sure we do."

"I never knew what he was doing up there," Mom adds. They're both trying hard.

"He was pretending he was Superboy," I tell her. "Trying to fly. Remember? He called himself boy of steel."

Dad turns to look at me. "You never told us that, Chase. We've always wondered."

"What are you talking about? You saw him."

"No, we heard you shout his name, heard him fall. When we came out, he was on the ground."

"He wore a towel like a cape."

"I don't remember a cape," Mom says. "I remember you crying. We could see his arm was broken. When we asked what happened, you said he fell. You never told us he said anything."

One-two-three-four. Two-four-six-eight. "But you saw him. You heard him say it."

"Look at me, Chase! I'm Superboy!"

Breathe. "You *heard* him—"

I see myself at the age of nine standing at a door.

"Chase, is something wrong?" Dad.

"No. I'm fine." I lean back in my seat.

"I'm sorry we don't remember it the way you do."

"That's okay."

My parents look at each other again.

At school I keep an eye out for Darla. Hoping for the opportunity to tell her how sorry I am. What a bastard I was. I want to show her a different person. A confident one.

On my way to eighth period I see her heading toward me, head down. "Hey."

She looks up, surprised. "Hi, Chase." She starts to walk around me.

"Wait, can I talk to you a minute?" I ask.

"Not right now."

"After school, then. I'll walk with you."

"I've gotta get home right after school."

"Oh."

"My dad's home."

"Really? For how long?"

"Look, I've got study hall at the other end of the building, but if you make it quick . . . What do you want to talk about?"

Now I can't think what to say. I want to say just the

right thing. "I'm feeling a lot better," I tell her. "I'd like to tell you about it."

She puts her hand on my shoulder. "I'm glad, Chase. I really am. But I've gotta go."

As I watch her retreat, I realize I didn't apologize, and I start to call out. But there are too many kids in the hall, and she's hurrying away, almost running. Is she trying to get away from me?

Heather's back. In drama she makes a point of showing everybody the bruise below her eye. Except me.

Mom's actually home when I get there, and she's made a chocolate pie. I eat a piece even though I'm not hungry, and we sit at the table and actually talk about my day. By the time I go up to my room, I've decided it feels good to have my parents fussing over me. Even if it's because they're worried I might go off the deep end.

Lying on the bed, I start thinking about Darla. Irritated that it seemed more important to her to get away from me than let me make amends.

I wonder how long her dad's home for? How long until he has to go out on his next job?

"You might as well have just called her a whore." The voice was right. I was horrible to her. I still haven't told her I'm sorry.

"Come here, Chase, I've got something to show you."

I sit up. Take a couple of deep breaths.

One-two-three-four. Two-four-six-eight. Breathe.

I feel better.

I'll make sure I apologize to her at school tomorrow.

Or I could call her right now.

I pull out the phone book, then realize since she's new in the area, her number won't be in it. Information gives me two listings for Prince, along with addresses.

The first one, listed to a Betty Prince, rings ten times before a woman's voice comes on the line. "Hello?"

"May I speak to Darla, please?"

"What? Can you borrow what?"

"Darla," I say louder. "Can I speak to Darla, please?"

"No, I don't want any magazines. Leave me alone!" She hangs up.

I dial L. Prince.

After four rings a male voice answers. "Hello?"

My voice falters.

"Hello?" the voice says. "Is someone there?"

"May I speak to Darla?" I ask in a raspy voice.

"She's not here right now."

"Oh." I glance at the address.

"Do you want to leave a message?"

I clear my voice, but it still comes out hoarse. "Do you know when she'll be home?"

"She went down the street a minute."

"I'll call back another time." I hang up.

That was stupid. I begin pacing the room. I know where her street is. I can see the look on her face, though. "You walked all the way over here to tell me what?"

I'll do it tomorrow.

But the thought of waiting causes a knot in my stomach. I can't shake the feeling that something's wrong and I've got to make it right.

"Come here, Chase, I've got something to show you."

I see myself at the age of nine standing at a door. Scared to death. Because I know what's on the other side.

I can't go over there now. I'll talk to her tomorrow.

For the rest of the night it feels like my stomach wants to burst. Mom almost catches me checking the crucifix.

Before dinner Dad and I go rent a movie. Mom fixes my favorite foods. I let them talk me into a game of Silver Screen Trivial Pursuit after the movie's over.

For the first time since we started playing the game, I lose.

CHAPTER 16

Darla's not at school. I decide to go to her house after my last class. I have my appointment, but based on the address from telephone information, Darla's house is about a mile and a half from school, and less than a mile from Dr. Braun's office. If I hurry, I can stop by Darla's and be no more than a few minutes late for therapy.

After school I start walking. Twenty minutes later I turn onto her street. The neighborhood doesn't look any different from mine. A typical suburb.

I find the address on a mailbox by the curb. The house is small but nice. With a garden in the front yard and a small white fence. Shades on the windows. A flowerpot on a windowsill.

At the door I take a deep breath and knock. My heart is a wrecking ball swinging against my chest.

I see myself at the age of nine standing at a door—

The door opens, and a woman—her mother, I guess—stares at me. "Can I help you?"

"I'm here to see Darla."

"Oh." I expect her to ask, *Are you the guy who hurt my daughter's feelings?*

Instead she smiles and says, "Just a minute. I'll get her."

I fidget while I wait.

The front door wide open.

And suddenly . . .

I see myself at the age of nine standing at a door.

. . . memories come, fast and furious.

I'm flying. Then I hit—

"There was a witness, if you remember." Dr. Braun. *"She says the car that hit you came from around the corner so fast there was no way Angie had time to react. It's good you fell out or you would have been killed—"*

I see myself at the age of nine—

"Chase?"

Come here, Chase. I've got something to show—

"What are you doing here?"

"I feel like we're dealing with fragments here." Dr. Braun again. *"Pieces that, by themselves, are hard to understand. But if we could figure out how they fit together in just the right way . . ."*

"Chase, is something wrong?"

I see myself—

"Darla." How long has she been there? "Darla, I . . . I came to . . ."

She steps out, closes the door, and I feel a tremendous pressure lifted off me. "Sit down," she offers. "You looked for a minute like you were going to faint.

"How'd you find my house?" she asks.

"Information."

"What are you doing here?"

"You weren't at school today."

"So?"

I feel stupid, but I plow forward. "You left so abruptly yesterday. I didn't get to apologize. I acted like a jerk when I . . . you know. I'm sorry. I'm really sorry."

"Are you sure you're okay?"

"Yeah."

"I'm glad you're here, actually. There's something I need to tell you."

"What?"

"I'm moving."

She says it so matter-of-factly, I don't understand at first. "You're what?"

"Dad was at his company's Florida office, and they offered him a position. A good one. He won't have to travel anymore."

"You . . . You're going to Florida?"

"Yes," Darla says, smiling. "He'll have an office and be finished at five every day. With weekends off and everything."

"You're leaving? Just like that?"

"Not 'just like—'"

"You're leaving 'cause of me."

"Jesus Christ, Chase. Why would you think . . ." She hesitates. Then says, in a gentler tone, "No. It has nothing to do with you and me."

"I'm sorry. I just can't believe . . ." I start to stand, then sit back down. "It's so fast."

"Listen." Darla looks at me. "I should explain. Tell you what Heather was talking about. I probably owe you that."

"You don't owe—"

"Just listen." She takes a deep breath. "What she said was true. I went through a period in my life when . . . well . . ." She shrugs. "I was a slut. I'm not proud of it. But I'm not gonna apologize for it either."

She pauses. "My parents were going through a rough time. They were even talking divorce. My dad was gone a lot, and they weren't communicating much when he was home. It got so bad that, a year ago, when Dad left on this one assignment, Mom and I didn't know if he was coming back. I was scared. I met this girl at my last school, and we became friends. Good friends, I thought. I cared for her. More than I'd cared for anybody. I could really talk to her. I liked being . . . *close* to her . . . and I thought she felt the same way toward me.

"One day she told me she didn't want to see me anymore. I was miserable. Dad was gone. I didn't know if my parents were splitting up, and this girl who I thought loved me . . . hurt me in a way I'd never been hurt before. Word was, I was a lesbian. She told everyone our friendship ended because I came on to her.

"I got angry. And took it out on myself. I slept around. Different guys. What Heather told you was true. I wish it wasn't . . ."

She wavers. "My dad came back. My parents talked and decided to try and work it out. We came with him when his job moved him here. My dad still had to travel a lot, but my parents were really working on their marriage.

"I asked myself, was I homosexual? Bisexual? Was it just a phase? I still don't know. It may sound weird, but that's why I dress the way I do. And why I didn't want to be more physical with you, Chase. I didn't want to give myself that way to someone until I was sure of who I was. I'm sorry if that hurt you. Being the new kid a lot, I've always felt like I had to redefine myself. When I came here, I decided I didn't want to do that anymore. And I didn't care if anyone understood."

"And now?" I ask quietly.

"Now that we're going someplace permanent, maybe I can just be myself." She shrugs. "Whatever that is."

"Where in Florida?"

"Saint Petersburg." She tries a smile. "Can you see me lying on a beach?"

"When are you leaving?"

"Day after tomorrow."

"Day after—So soon?"

"Yes," she says.

"I'm gonna miss you."

"I'll miss you, too."

"I don't want you to go."

"Chase . . ."

I struggle to find something magical to say that might keep her here. "I really am sorry for the way I acted."

"I know."

More silence. "I'm sorry I'm not gonna get to meet your brother."

I glance at her but say nothing.

For some reason my mother's words from our conversation the other night come back to me. *We prayed every night Ben would be safe.*

"You're the most sensitive guy I've ever met, Chase."

Echoing in my head. *"We prayed every night . . ."*

"You deserve a lot more than someone like Heather."

"*. . . every night . . .*"

"I hope you know that."

"*. . . Ben would be safe.*"

"*. . . safe.*"

I see him standing on the roof, arms spread wide, like the arms of Jesus on the crucifix.

"*Look at me, Chase! I'm Superboy! Boy of steel!*"

"Chase?"

Falling forward.

"*Boy of—*"

"He didn't say it!"

Darla looks at me. "What?"

I stand up. "I always told myself he did, but . . . he didn't. He just fell. I saw him."

"*Do it! Cut your lousy wrists!*"

"But I didn't know what was going on. Not till later."

I'm flying. Then I hit—

"I should have said something . . ."

"*We prayed every night Ben would be safe.*"

I see myself standing at a—

"He *wasn't* safe!" I scream. "He told me he was okay, but he wasn't. I should have—"

"Chase, you're scaring me!" Darla stands. "What the hell are you talking about?"

"I have to go."

"Go? But there's something else I wanted to tell you."

I waver; look back. "What?"

"Even though I'm moving," she says, "I was hoping we'd still be friends."

Just like Angie. *"I'm still your friend."*

And Ben. *"I love you."*

"Maybe we can keep in touch."

Are those tears I see in her eyes? "I've gotta go."

"Where?"

"I have an appointment." What time is it? Will Dr. Braun wait for me if I'm late?

"Chase—"

"I love you. I'm sorry."

"What? What did you . . ."

But I don't hear the rest. I only hear and feel and see the whirling images in my head threatening to pull me apart as I start to run.

I'm . . . flying . . .

Faster, unable to escape the images.

. . . standing at a door.

One-two-three-four. Stop!

Scared to death.

Faster.

Because I know . . .

Two-four-six-eight. Make it stop!

. . . what's on the other side.

CHAPTER 17

Her office door is open when I rush into the waiting room. She comes out, takes one look, and says, "Chase, what is it?"

"I'm late."

"I know."

"I'm sorry."

"It's okay. What's wrong?"

"I can't . . ."

"Can't what?"

"Make it stop. I try, but I can't."

"Let's go inside and talk about it."

Inside, Dr. Braun leads me to my usual seat and pulls her chair up close.

"Whatever it is," she says, "you're safe now. I'm

not going anywhere. Tell me what happened."

"I went to see Darla," I say. "She's moving away."

"Your friend in drama?"

"Her dad got a job in Florida."

"Is this why you're so upset?"

"I'm upset because . . ." I choke. Can't talk.

"Let me help you. You said you couldn't make it stop."

"I can't."

"What can't you stop?"

"The door. It's locked, but I know he's in there."

"Who?"

"He told me not to worry about it."

"Tell me who you're talking about."

"Ben. I though he said he was *Superboy.* Boy of steel. But I was wrong. He didn't say it. I don't know why I thought . . ."

"Go on. I'm listening."

"Later, when I found out . . . he said he had it under control. He made me promise not to say anything to Mom and Dad. I didn't. I kept my word. But I should have told. Mom told me she and Dad used to pray Ben would be safe. But he wasn't. I knew he wasn't."

Dr. Brown raises her head, a look of awful awareness on her face. "Because something was happening to Ben?"

"On the other side of the door."

"How old were you?"

"Nine."

"And Ben was eleven. The age he was when he jumped off the roof."

I nod my head.

"What's on the other side of that door?"

"I . . . I can't . . ."

"Okay," she says. "Try describing the door to me."

"Describe—?"

"What color is it?"

"Dark brown."

"What about the doorknob?"

"Gold."

"You can't get in?"

"No. It's locked from the inside. I don't have a key."

"Anything else? Maybe something *on* the door?"

I falter, then whisper, "Jesus."

"Jesus?"

"The crucifix in our living room. My dad has it now. Cherishes it. Jesus on the cross. It hangs above the mantel in our living room."

"This crucifix has been in your family for a long time?"

"Yes. I have to keep checking it. Dad would get so upset if it was broken. I'm sorry I didn't tell you. That's who said 'do it.'"

"The voice you heard just before you cut your wrists came from this figure of Jesus?"

"I didn't know until . . . I was leaving to take the money to Ben."

"That's who you were arguing with when your parents walked in."

I nod my head.

"And before your father had it, the crucifix was mounted on this locked door you can't get through?"

Again, I nod.

"Who's door was it?"

She has to lean forward to hear me. "My uncle's."

"Your dad's brother."

"Yes. He had it on his bedroom door. He lived next door to us. He was twelve years older than my dad. His picture's on the mantel with the other family pictures. He's dead now."

"How did he die?"

"Uncle Julius had some lung disease," I explain.

"Is that why he lived next door?"

"Yes. So we could help him. One of Ben's chores was to go there three times a week, clean up the house, keep our uncle company."

"And when Ben couldn't go because of his arm . . ."

"Dad said I had to."

Dr. Braun leans forward, takes my hand. "I want you to tell me about that, Chase. But before you start, remember—you're safe here. No matter what you tell me, nothing is going to happen. Do you believe me?"

I stare into her eyes. After a moment, I nod.

"Okay, then." She takes a deep breath. "Now tell me what's on the other side of that door."

"Look at me, Chase! I'm Superboy!"

"Ben, oh my God, please come down from there."

"Son, you climb back into the window right now. Right now! Do you hear me?"

Only it doesn't happen that way. Walking out of the house, I hear nothing, but look up and see him standing there, wearing no cape, just a strange, hollow look on his face as he spreads his arms and pitches forward off the roof, making me cry out.

It could have been worse. The doctor says his arm will heal in four to six weeks. In the meantime, Dad tells me, at nine, I'm old enough to pitch in and do some of my older brother's chores. Including going over to Uncle Julius's house.

"I'll give you an extra five dollars' allowance," he promises.

I tell him, sure. Eager for five extra dollars every week. Eager to show how grown-up I am.

The first three weeks go fine. Housework includes bagging up newspapers, filling the dishwasher and running it, emptying trash cans, and generally sweeping up. My uncle can get around the house if he wants, but he spends a lot of the time watching television. Game shows and afternoon reruns of old shows like *Gilligan's Island* and *The Andy Griffith Show*. He likes it when I watch TV with him. He's a big man who, before he got sick, would laugh and bray like the boys in the Disney *Pinocchio* when they change into donkeys. Ben and I used to joke with each other about that laugh. And about the way his breath smelled, like stale cigarettes and the fruity wine Mom and Dad allowed themselves occasionally. He always brought gifts the two times a year he visited. Great gifts, expensive gifts that made my mother frown and my father shake his head, smile, and say, "It's okay, Mary Beth, he's their uncle." Even as little kids, we could see how much Dad looked up to his brother, how Uncle Julius could do no wrong in his eyes.

The church Dad served then owned the house next to the parsonage, and when my uncle got sick, the church board gave permission to let him live there. After Ben got hurt, I started going twice a week.

Uncle Julius had a collection of old black-and-white movies on videotape and sometimes he and I watched those instead of regular TV. When a movie was over, we'd talk about it, and he'd tell me what a real movie buff I was, just like him. Sometimes he even let me take them home to watch. And sometimes he'd ask me questions like, what do I like to do for fun besides watch films, what do I do with my friends? Is Ben's arm healing okay, do I know when he's coming back? Maybe when he does, I can still keep coming over.

On my second visit of the fourth week, after my chores are done, he asks me to watch a tape with him. I see that, unlike the other tapes, this one has no label on it. "What's it called?" I ask.

"Just put it in the machine and come here next to me," he says from his bed.

I put the tape in and, right away, it starts to play. The first thing I notice is that it's in color, not like the old movies we watched before. And there's no loud music, no opening credits.

"Come sit with me, Chase," my uncle says, patting the space next to him. Not the chair where I usually sit. It feels weird, but I sit on the bed. Smiling, he says, "Now watch the movie."

Even as a nine-year-old, I can see how poor the quality of the film is. On the screen is an empty room. Then a man and a woman walk in. They talk. Then they begin to kiss. Then another man comes into the room behind the woman and begins touching her. And for the first time I feel Uncle Julius's hand on my arm. . . .

• • •

"What was on the tape, Chase?"

Almost a whisper, "Three people. Having sex."

"Did you understand then that's what it was?"

"A friend of mine played an R-rated movie at his house once when his parents weren't around. So I'd seen people kissing and taking their clothes off before."

"But this was more?"

I nod. "After the three people were finished, a lot more people came into the room."

"In the movie."

"Yes."

"And what was your uncle doing during this?"

"He had his hand on my arm. Then he takes my hand and starts to pull it toward him, but I yank it back. And he says, 'No, don't. It's okay. I need your help with something. Ben does it all the time. And more. Lots more. He's a big help.' He takes my hand again and keeps saying, 'It's okay. Ask Ben when you see him later, he'll tell you.' But we can't say anything. Not to anyone. Because some people would get mad and wouldn't let me come over to watch the old movies anymore. They would get mad at Ben and mad at me."

"Then what happened?"

"I got up to leave."

"And?"

"He calls to me . . ."

"Come here, Chase, I've got something to show you."

"I stop. Turn back around. I remember thinking, maybe he's just kidding and now he's gonna let me in on the joke. Start laughing like he always does."

"But?"

"He's pulled the blanket back. He's naked. He wants me . . . wants me to . . . I can't say it."

"That's all right. You don't have to tell me now."

"He keeps saying, 'It's all right. Ben does it. It's fun.'"

"Did he make you do what he wanted?"

"No. I ran away. I got out of there."

"Did you tell your parents?"

Silence.

"Chase?"

"No. I told Ben."

"I'm really sorry, Chase. Are you okay?"

"Yeah but, Ben, he said . . ."

"What?"

"He said you watch those movies with him."

"I do, Chase."

"He said you do other things."

"Chase, it's okay. I didn't know he was going to try . . . I'm sorry."

"You do those things? Those things he said?"

"I should never have let you go over there. I should have told

Mom and Dad my arm didn't matter. It's fine now. I'll go back to doing the chores there, and you won't have to go back anymore."

"But we have to tell Mom and Dad."

"No! We can't." He stares at me, his eyes as hard as I've ever seen them. *"Dad looked up to Uncle Julius when he was growing up. He still does. Do you know what it will do to him if we tell him? That's if he believed us. I don't think he would. It's better we don't say anything. Just keep things the way they are. I've got it under control. I can handle it."*

"But, Ben—"

"You've got to promise me you won't say anything, Chase."

"Ben—"

"I'm your brother. Promise me!"

Silence. "I promise, Ben."

"And you never said anything?"

"No."

"What happened to your dad's brother?"

"He died a year later."

"And your parents never knew."

"No. After my uncle was gone, Ben told me, again, not to say anything. But I should have. I knew why he kept getting into trouble. I know why he snapped on that old man he robbed."

"Tell me about the door again."

"I snuck over to Uncle Julius's the next time Ben was

there. The bedroom door was locked. But I heard things. Through the wood. After that, every time Ben went over, I snuck into the house. The bedroom door was always locked. With that figure of Jesus on it. And I knew."

"What did you know?"

"What was happening. And I didn't say anything."

"Why?"

"I promised Ben."

"Why else?"

Silence.

"You know."

Tears cloud my vision.

"It was like Ben said," Dr. Braun says in a subdued voice. "If you told them, they might not believe you. Then it'd be worse. Because your uncle would know you'd told. Then what would you do? Who would protect you?

"So you did the only thing you could. You kept the secret."

I hesitate, then nod my head.

"But that's not the worst of it. Right?"

The room is closing in.

"Come on, Chase. It's okay to admit it now. The biggest, darkest secret. You didn't say anything because . . ."

Time stands still, the moment stretching out for

eternity. "Because . . . I knew . . . as long as he had Ben . . . he wouldn't come after me."

Now it has to happen. I wait for Dr. Braun to condemn me.

"That's a huge secret you've been keeping all these years," she says. "One you should never have had to keep."

"I should have—"

"No." She leans in. "Your uncle was a child abuser. People like him are very good at making their victims feel it's their fault because the victims are *children*. He abused your brother terribly. And he abused you, even if it didn't get to the level it did with Ben. It wasn't fair of Ben to ask you to keep his secret. But he was only eleven. The only person at fault was your uncle."

"But why did Ben feel he couldn't say anything?"

"We'll never know for sure, Chase. But you said it yourself. Ben protected you. Your brother obviously felt he couldn't go to your parents, especially your dad. And judging from the way they handled your brother's incarceration and death, I understand why. After surviving his fall from the roof, when you told him what happened with your uncle, he decided to protect you. In the only way he thought he could."

"I told myself he was indestructible."

"You saw him fall. Maybe somewhere deep inside, you realized he'd done it on purpose. But you didn't know why then. Much later, when the dream started, you came up with the 'Superboy' moniker as part of the memory rather than admit to the pain he'd been feeling. Pain you unfairly blamed yourself for."

Dr. Braun puts her hand on my arm. "When you think you're ready, I'd like you to talk about this here with your parents." I look at her. "I know that scares you, so just think about it. We have time. But it's important we do it eventually. It won't be easy. But they realize now the mistakes they've made. You might be surprised at how they react. They called earlier, and when I told them you weren't here yet, they sounded worried. We should call and tell them you're okay."

I sigh; nod my head.

"You grew up in an insecure environment. Your father served a number of churches and kept moving you around. Anything that would have stirred up the little stability you had, probably scared you to death. But what happened was not your fault. Even though you've been living your life like it was. As if you don't deserve anything good. Like your relationship with Angie.

"But Angie saw good in you. Even after she ended the relationship, she still came to pick you up when you and your friends got too drunk to drive."

She drives up, and we're all laughing. Dan Butler and Sara Buchanan and Jay Kerrigan.

And me.

"Even though you've never been able to see it in yourself."

Angie shakes her head. Smiles. I end up in the front seat.
"Thanks for coming, Angie."

"You're welcome."

"Do you remember something about the accident now?"

"Angie picking us up."

"Anything else?"

"No."

"Think back. You've blanked it out because of something that happened inside that car. Something that went against this terrible image you have of yourself all because of a promise you made to your brother."

"I don't know . . ."

"She took the time to come out in the middle of the night to get you. What is she, some kind of saint? Doesn't she know how worthless you are?"

Somebody makes a joke—it's Dan, not me—and we laugh. Angie, too. And then the headlights seem to come from out of nowhere, filling the inside of the car.

"Right up to the end, she refused to believe that about you. Didn't she?"

Things happen in slow motion.

"What is it, Chase?"

Angie turns toward me with that look on her face . . .

"You remember now, don't you?"

"No."

. . . knowing she's going to die . . .

"Yes, you do. What happened during the accident that was so horrible, you blocked it out?"

. . . but she reaches toward me . . .

"Please don't make me—"

. . . and . . .

"Chase . . ."

I'm flying . . .

"Tell me!"

"She *pushed* me!"

Silence.

Then again, "She pushed me."

Dr. Braun waits.

"It happened so quickly. Suddenly the other car's just there. Angie tried to swerve, but we were going to hit it anyway. I see that awful look on her face, then she's reaching toward me . . ."

"Are you sure she was reaching?"

"What?"

"Or did the impact push her against you?"

"I . . . I don't understand . . ."

"What about the door?" Dr. Braun asks.

"I was so drunk, I must not have closed it all the way."

"So the impact probably popped it open *and* knocked her against you, and you fell out."

"No. She . . . she must have seen the door was open and . . . saved my life."

"I doubt there was time for her to notice the door was partly open and *then* push you out."

"No!" I shout, crying now. "Why are you saying that?"

"Chase, what matters is that everyone in that car deserved to survive, including you. The others didn't survive. That's horrible and unfair. But you *did* survive. And that's a *good* thing."

"I . . . I don't know . . ."

Dr. Braun pulls her chair next to mine, puts her arm around me. "Listen to me, Chase. It's okay now. All the secrets are out. Even the one you thought you had to keep from yourself. We're going to talk about this. A lot. But the hardest part's over. Now you can truly start to heal."

Later, after we've called my parents, then talked some more, it's Dr. Braun's promise that she'll be here for me in the days to come that allows me to leave her office and go out into the night, where Mom and Dad wait to drive me home. Tomorrow, when daylight comes, it will shine on a whole new terrible world for me. One without Ben or Angie. Or Darla.

For now, I'm grateful for the darkness.